I0717866

Holiday From Hell

DEMELZA CARLTON

DEDICATION

*For my husband, who first took me to Margaret River on
our honeymoon.
This dedication comes with his warning:
Never trust Lucifer. Sympathy for the devil will cause
nothing but trouble.*

One

Tears streamed freely down Keiko's face. "It was an honour to have met you, Mere-san. I only wish you could have stayed longer."

Mel caught Koyane's fleeting smile and tried not to laugh at the siren's disappointment. She leaned close to the girl and hugged her. "If you want something from the Indian Ocean, you must first offer their leader, Sirena, a favour that creates a deep debt. Send your brother to provide a service that no one else can."

The girl's eyes shone, unshed tears shimmering over her resurrected smile. "Thank you, Mere-san."

"You already have my gratitude, Murielle-sama, and my deepest apologies for taking your precious time when you are needed elsewhere." Koyane lowered his eyes and bowed deeply again. Mel could feel his shame at the need to call for help.

She touched his cheek, not breaking the contact as he straightened to face her. "I help where it is needed. There is no shame in it. None of us are perfect. Thank you for your care and hospitality. I hope we may meet for longer next time." It was her turn to bow, though just a shallow bob of her head.

"Be well, take care and travel safe, Mere-san," Koyane replied. He hesitated, then added, "Please convey my well-wishes to your fallen angel and my hopes that next time you grace my house, you will allow me to extend my hospitality to him, too."

"Thank you, Koyane. It was a pleasure to work with you again. *Go-kuro sama desu. Osaki ni shitsurei shimasu.*" (Thank you for a job well done. I am sorry to leave you with work still to do.)

"*Osaki ni shiturei itashimasu.*" (Thank you for all your hard work.)

The formal farewells said, Mel headed through the departure gate. Security, ticket and passport checks progressed quickly and she soon found herself outside the duty free shops in the departure lounge.

"Miss?" Mel glanced up to meet the eyes of the uniformed airport hostess. "Your lounge is this way." The girl gestured at a set of doors to Mel's left.

Mel thanked her and slipped into the shop that sold her perfume. If Luce was using it to scent the bed linen in her home, she'd need another bottle or perhaps two. Not to mention a bottle of some lovely Japanese whiskey to share with Luce.

Fifteen minutes later, the sealed duty free bag clutched in her hand, Mel sank into one of the business lounge armchairs. A waitress brought her a pot of green tea and Mel settled down to enjoy the last hour before her flight home to Luce.

Time flew and Mel roused at the sound of her boarding call. Time to go home.

The steward who took her ticket ushered her to a first class seat and Mel smothered her laughter. Patrick, Luce and now Koyane were conspiring to give her unaccustomed luxury, but they were correct that her body required such pampering right now. In her present state of health, she needed to sleep on this flight.

She glanced at the dinner menu as the plane left the runway, smiling as she noticed the oysters Luce would have ordered if he was by her side, as he should be. Soon.

Mel managed to finish the little entrée tart and most of her lobster main course, but she waved away the offer of dessert. All she wanted was a cup of milk and sleep, she thought as she watched the steward make up her bed. She mumbled something about being woken for breakfast in time to eat before the plane landed and the steward seemed to understand. More exhausted than she could ever remember being before, she crept into her bed and slept, promising herself that the next time she closed her eyes, she'd be in Luce's arms.

Two

Mel waved to the taxi driver as she headed into the HELL Corporation building. She'd timed her arrival perfectly between the lunchtime crush and the mid-afternoon coffee crowd, so she slipped into the near-empty office without anyone noticing until she passed Mephi's desk.

Mephi's relieved smile set her on edge. "Thank Heaven you're back. It's been Hell here without you," Luce's PA breathed.

Glancing at Luce's empty office, Mel asked, "Where is he?"

"Giving a presentation to all staff in the seminar room. I only got out of it because someone had to take his calls. When did you get back?" She eyed Mel's suitcase. "Did you come here straight from the airport?"

Mel laughed. "Yes. I figured I was needed here."

Mephi dropped her voice to a barely audible whisper. "Go home. Take a shower and a rest and unpack. The trouble here can wait. I'll tell him you'll be in tomorrow. You don't need to deal with Lord Prick today. He's been nothing short of impossible since he got back. Don't wear a skirt to work tomorrow – I've never seen a man more frustrated, in more ways than one. And when he's the Lord of Hell…well, he's the devil of a man who always gets his desires. Don't make it easy for him."

It hurt to hear Luce described in such unflattering terms, but Mephi didn't know Luce like Mel did. "I'm sure I can handle him."

"That's what he wants. And I think he'd sell his soul to handle you, so watch out," Mephi said darkly.

Mel bobbed her head as she had to Koyane

in the airport. "Thank you for the warning. I'd best be going, then."

Once out of the executive offices, she knew exactly where to go – Mephi's warning be damned. She hadn't come home to wait another day to see him.

Mel approached the closed seminar room doors. She could hear Luce's voice booming as he reprimanded someone. Her thoughts darted to her first media conference in this room. She didn't want to fall to her knees, speechless, on the stairs again. Focussing on her breathing, Mel decided to wait a few minutes until she was perfectly calm.

She heard the doors open and close. Footsteps padded on the carpet.

"Don't go in. Get out before he sees you. Go back to Heaven, or at least as far away from him as you can, so he can't find you, Mel. Please," Merih said, looking pained. "He doesn't deserve you and he has no right to keep you prisoner again. Escape while you can. I'll tell him I never saw you."

Mel managed a smile of sympathy for his pain. "I'm no one's prisoner, and Luce has no hold over me. Has he really been that bad?"

Merih nodded, biting his lip. "Since he got back from his last business trip. I've never seen him this angry – not in centuries. You should go."

"I'll go in. I need to know how bad this is," Mel said, pressing her hand to the door.

"If he does anything to hurt you, I swear we'll stage a mutiny," Merih muttered.

Mel pushed the door open and stepped into the seminar room. From the look of it, a mutiny was already underway. The room was full of shouting demons, standing and shaking fists at Luce.

Luce was in fine form behind the lectern, his tail swishing as he bellowed, "If you don't follow my orders, I'll…" He broke off to stare at Mel. "Melody," he breathed.

The demons fell silent as they followed his gaze, but they stayed standing. Mel felt her knees weakening, but she forced herself not to fall. It wasn't public speaking if she knew everyone, she told herself.

Help me, Luce's eyes said.

How could she refuse such a desperate plea?

Mel trotted down the steps to Luce's side, saying, "What briefing am I late for?" She glanced at the projector screens. "Ooh, did the new records management software finally arrive? That system is nothing short of miraculous. Instead of having to print out all your correspondence, punch it and file it in every relevant paper file, you just click a button with your mouse and it's filed automatically. You can even schedule your computer to do it for you." She covered a smile with her fingers as she laid her other hand on top of Luce's. "I heard the best time to schedule it is when you want a long coffee break, because it can take half an hour or so for the computer to process correspondence and it locks your computer up nicely while it's busy, so you can't do anything else on it until it's done. We might have to order more coffee, or we'll run out mid-week." She surveyed the room, where demons were backing down and some were even resuming their seats. "Didn't you get to that bit yet?" She grinned impishly up at Luce. "Sorry. I should take a seat and behave for the rest of the briefing, right?"

"It's finished," Luce said, his voice growling in his throat. His claws dug into the lectern laminate as he clenched those big, red fingers. "Everyone should get back to work." In the noisy mass exodus, he added, "You should go home and rest, Mel. HELL is no place for an angel like you who's off saving the world every other day. You shouldn't be here."

Mel waited for the last demon to leave before she said, "Yes, I should. I've missed you, Luce." She touched her lips to his in a gentle kiss before she glanced down. "I must admit, you look pretty happy to see me, too. So, when did you stop wearing pants to the office? You're hardly keeping a low profile among humans in this form."

He looked uncomfortable. "The imps made an illusion so humans see me as just a man in a suit. The demons…they're restless and insubordinate. Looking like this, I can still scare them into following orders. Most of the time. It's so *hard*, Mel. I don't know what's happening." He sank to the floor, his head in his hands.

Mel dropped to her knees beside him. "It's a

good thing I'm home early to help you, then." She spread her arms wide in an invitation.

He grasped her in a desperate hug, pressing his face against her breast. "God, Mel, you don't know how good it is to see you again. I'm so sorry for messing up in Japan. I thought I was helping, but I just don't know how to do what you do. It's so much easier to slip into my old ways and I feel like it'll take forever for me to learn enough to be able to help you. And that woman…God, that woman…I didn't even want to touch her. I was trying to help you, if you can believe that."

"I know. Truly I know. You meant well, Luce, which is what matters. The consequences…ah, humans have free will. They can always reject what I have to offer and accept what's worst for them." She pressed her lips to the top of his head, kissing the sensitive skin at the base of each of his horns as her fingers stroked the hot, red skin down his spine. Did he have any idea how soothing the contact was for her? "I never realised how much I'd miss you, my love. It hurt not to have you with me. We're together now. I'll help you put this place right. Everything will work out for the best – I promise."

He tilted his head up. "You're such a sweet angel, Mel. Too good for me, but I don't know what I'd do without you." He kissed her with passion and need so thick she could taste it. Her exhaustion seemed to lift like a fading fog as the warmth of his love flooded her soul. It wasn't possible – souls couldn't directly share energy like this, surely. She'd never heard of such a thing…but she'd never bonded with another soul, either. Was it the bond they shared or simply the power of Luce's love for her? He wasn't just healing her body – he was restoring her soul. The air around them had a distinct ripple in its energy, just like the disturbance she'd noticed in Patrick's flat when they'd been talking about her trip through Hell. What if…

The door at the top of the steps swung open and shut, so quickly and silently that Luce didn't seem to notice. Mel wondered who had seen their intimate exchange, but she dismissed the thought. Luce needed her now – his minions didn't matter for the moment.

"First, you need to present an image that's far more in control than you are now," Mel began, concentrating on his body. Under her fingers, his ruddy skin paled to a light tan, softening with every stroke. "Still sexy, but you should be wearing a suit, not simply an illusion of one." Her eyes lingered on the naked man in her arms, before she clothed him carefully. "I'm sorry, I can't do black – just grey. If you really want to look dark and demonic, you'll have to fix that." She rose and stretched her hand out. "If you wish to accompany me, you'll have to rise with me, my love. I'm planning on spending the afternoon relaxing – anywhere but here. No matter what state it's in, your corporation can wait, for I won't do any more for it today. What's your afternoon schedule look like?"

Luce grinned and grasped her hand, leaping lightly to his feet. The suave, suited CEO brushed imaginary dust from his jacket. "You know I'm at your command. For you…I'll happily wipe my desk and my schedule clean. I'll phone Mephi and tell her I'm taking the rest of the day off." He whipped his phone out of his back pocket and Mel wondered where he'd kept it when he wasn't wearing pants. "Unless you'd like to book a very long afternoon meeting. We can lock my office door, I can lay you on the desk, fall to my knees and thank you properly for being my angel, for simply being here…and anything else I can think of."

"I'll pass on the dirty desk, Luce. Take me home."

Three

"Here, let me take that." Luce lifted Mel's suitcase out of the car and wheeled it along behind him, holding out his free hand for Mel's. Just the warmth of her fingers laced through his was a taste of Heaven. He tightened his grip on her, not wanting to let go.

The trip up to his penthouse seemed interminable, but Luce endured it until he could kick the door shut behind them. Alone at last.

"Where would you like to relax? The bed,

the sofa…up against the front door? Your wish is my command." Luce grinned, loosening his tie.

Mel laughed merrily. "Why your mind goes straight to sex, I will never understand. I was thinking about swans." She slipped off her shoes. "I'd like to take a leisurely walk to go feed the swans. I stopped in at the bakery downstairs from your office, so I have the dark, seedy rolls they like, and, now I have you all afternoon, I want to take you with me."

Sighing inwardly, Luce adjusted himself. Maybe she'd be up for sex later. An idea sparked and he said, "How about we head down to the foreshore where we had the Christmas party last year? That swan you kissed is probably pining away for you."

Mel sank onto the tiles, fishing through her suitcase for what turned out to be a pair of sneakers and some socks. "Or he's bragged to every swan he knows about the tasty CEO he sampled and he's hanging out for more." She laughed at the look on his face. "Don't worry, Luce, I'll protect you. I think Matilda Bay is a wonderful idea. You might want to get changed into something a little more casual, though."

Luce hurried to do just that, finishing with lacing up his black sneakers before he said, "Let's go feed my fingers to the swans."

Mel laughed as she took his hand and they headed downstairs together. The light breeze pulled wisps of hair from Mel's braid and the spring sunlight turned the loose strands into a glowing halo. Even the weather wanted to caress his perfect angel.

The café was closing as they reached it, but Mel didn't seem to mind. She led the way to the same bench they'd used at the office Christmas party and Luce wasn't surprised when she tucked her skirt beneath her to sit in precisely the same spot where he'd found her feeding the swans then. A drift of swans by the river's edge turned their heads to stare at her, but only one ambled over.

Mel shredded a roll to beak-sized pieces in her lap and fed them one by one to the black bird. Luce couldn't keep his eyes off her joyful smile. Hell, how he'd missed her. He stretched his arm along the table behind her, then curled it around her shoulders. Mel was too enraptured by the swan to notice.

Luce sighed. "Are you going to kiss him again, too, to make me insanely jealous?" The swan tipped its beak up to swallow the last chunk of roll.

Mel's fingers caressed Luce's cheek and he looked into her eyes, startled, before she sealed his lips with a kiss, her lips parting to welcome his tongue. She sighed happily. "No, my love. I'm only going to kiss you today, to make us both happy."

Luce pulled her close, as eager as Mel for more heartfelt kisses. "My sweet, sweet Melody," he murmured, cupping her face in his hands. "There's no Heaven without you – only Hell."

He felt her discomfort before she pulled away. "You're making me sound more than I am, Luce. I'm not..."

He seized her hands. "You are. To me, you're Heaven. You're my bright, shining hope – since the first time we sat here together. You said dark wings don't make a demon. You saw through the illusions to my soul, Mel. You held me, healed me, looked deep inside me…and instead of turning and running away like anyone else would, you held my hands and looked deeper still until you cried for me. You said there was still light in my soul – you saw it! – and you gave me hope. Hope that life could be more than Hell because for the first time, I didn't want to see an angel fall. I wanted to see you rise."

Tears flowed silently down her cheeks, but they couldn't dampen her loving smile. "Luce…"

"I wanted to take you home with me, so I could be alone with you. Not…not just for sex…okay, maybe a bit. But I wanted…I wanted you as an angel. I didn't want you to fall because I wanted something to aspire to. I didn't know it then, but you're my salvation." He closed his eyes. "The reason I came to the party here was to seduce you. With a few words and your gentle hands, instead it was you who laid me bare – in front of demons, humans and an archangel who'd destroy me if she had the chance. You could have given me up to them, but you didn't. I still don't know why."

Mel pressed her hand to his chest, over his heart. "I took a fancy to your soul, my love, and I wanted it all to myself." Her eyes danced with laughter.

He stared at her. "Careful – you sound like me, or like I used to. If you're not careful, you'll be bargaining for souls just like a demon – and you'll put your own in danger. More than ever, I don't want to see you fall, Mel."

She let out a peal of laughter. "Luce, angels collect souls as readily as any demon. The difference is we don't bargain. We only take those souls that are given freely. The reward...ah, that comes after." She winked.

He didn't hesitate. "Mine's already yours – has been since the day we first sat here together. I need no reward – your friendship – companionship – whatever it is we have, is more than enough. More than I could have hoped for. I'm still deep in your debt – anything you ask for, I'll give you." His eyes bored into hers, desperate for her to accept everything he had to offer. Not to reject him – even after all the mistakes he'd made.

Her laughter died as her expression took on a more serious cast. "Thank you, Luce. You offer me...an amazing gift, and I fully appreciate your worth. I hope never to ask for more than you're willing to give." She took his hands and kissed them ceremoniously.

He held her hands for a long moment, wanting to savour the connection between them, before he said, "Can I ask you something personal?"

"Of course," she replied warmly.

He hesitated for a moment, but ploughed on with, "It's something Patrick, your...friend...in London, mentioned that I've been wondering about." A slight wariness crept into her expression, but she nodded, as if encouraging him to continue. "He said that here – this city – is where you come to rest between your more difficult diplomatic interventions. Where you don't spend all your time saving the world from...well, from me and Hell's other denizens."

"I work with humans, trying to save them from themselves," Mel corrected. "I'd never really spent much time working with or against demons until my first day at the HELL Corporation. When I last saw Patrick, I'd been working in HELL for a very short time and I was feeling a little overwhelmed. And then there was you – the puzzling demon who wasn't a demon, with your fascinating soul that I couldn't stop thinking about."

Luce perked up. "You were thinking about me while you were on holiday with him?"

He'd missed her laughter so much, so it was a joy to hear it bubble up in her throat again before she said, "Not like that. Honestly, Luce...I was worried about you. Not the same thing at all."

Dismissing her denial, Luce continued, "You said that HELL could wait a bit for you to set it to rights. I'm wondering how long you'd be willing to delay. A couple of weeks or maybe even a month? I want to make sure you've had a chance to rest before you delve into the deep-seated problems of a demonic corporation." He gripped her hands tighter when it felt like she'd pull away from him. "You're home early because you need rest, aren't you? Please say you'll let work wait."

"It could wait a month, if it had to," Mel began cautiously, "but just the thought of you enduring thirty days like today without me helping you...Luce, I couldn't be so selfish as to stay home when I know you're stressed and hurting."

"I won't," he replied eagerly. "I'll take the time off with you because I know you need it. I want to take you on a holiday. Just the two of us. No demons, no angels, no work – for a whole month. I rely on you more and more for sorting out the corporation's problems when I should let you rest. I don't want you to avoid coming here because there's more work for you to do. I miss you when you're away and I want to give you the kind of respite you need right here. You won't have to worry about anything – I'll take care of every detail. What do you say – do you trust me to give you the most relaxing holiday you've ever had?"

The wistful look in her eyes told him he had her convinced. For a moment, Luce felt her exhaustion as she sagged in his arms. She needed this – but she never considered her own needs.

"It sounds wonderful, Luce. But four weeks seems like too much – more than I need. One week is plenty, surely..."

His hands tightened around hers. "Humans get four weeks of holidays a year in this city and you work harder than any of them. I need this break as much as you do. Please, Mel. I'll make some calls this afternoon and you can leave the next month up to me."

She closed her eyes. "All right. On one condition."

"Name it, Melody. I'd do anything for you – you know that."

Mel's wicked smile sent his heart racing. "You make your calls and arrangements tomorrow, not today. Today, I was hoping you'd join me for dinner in a restaurant that does oysters just the way you like them. For tonight, you're going to need them."

Luce grinned. His angel had been thinking about sex – or maybe just reading his mind. "I'll call ahead and have dinner delivered to our apartment. After that...your wish is my command and it'll be a pleasure indeed."

Four

The steamy shower screen blurred her body's silhouette, leaving him aching for Mel in more places than he felt should be capable of feeling anything. Without thinking, Luce stripped swiftly and opened the shower door. "May I join you?" he asked, eyeing the water cascading down her hair.

Mel lifted her eyes. "I was just finishing up, but if you want…"

Luce didn't wait. He stepped in behind her, clicked the door shut, and pulled her body tight against his.

She seemed to sense his inner turmoil as she laid a sympathetic hand on his arm. "What's wrong, my love?"

"I need you. I need to feel you close to me. I've missed you so much while you've been away, it's been a constant ache in my heart. What's this bond we have for, except leaving me bereft when you're not here?" He hated the lost sound of his voice.

"I've missed you, too, you know, but through the bond between us, I could reach out and sense your feelings if I needed to feel close to you. Can't you sense mine at all?" Mel squirmed in his arms until she could look into his eyes. "Luce, tell me you can feel how much I love you."

He tried. God, he tried. He didn't dare tell her how badly he'd failed, but the anguish in his eyes must have told her anyway.

Mel's fierce kiss brought with it the wave of sensation he'd sought. Now her love washed over him, enveloping him in welcoming warmth that brought tears to his eyes. "Melody…"

Her warmth vanished the moment his lips left hers, leaving him horribly alone, even with her in his arms.

"Hold on, Luce. Tell me what it felt like."

He struggled to find the right words. "Heaven. It felt like my first dawn in Heaven, where the first rays of world-warming sunlight touched me, followed by the full blaze of the sun accepting me as her own and a part of her. And then gone, plunged into icy cold rock that..." Luce's voice died, but it was too late. He'd already summoned the memory of his first fall into Hell.

Mel's voice was deep and calm. "Focus on the first part. Not your fall, my love. Dawn, the sun, the warmth...I hold it all in my heart for you. All you need to do is reach out to claim it and it will always be yours."

He reached – God, he reached – but it was like trying to grasp the slippery bar of soap. No, harder than that. Like trying to catch a squirt of Mel's shower gel in just his fingers. He clutched her closer. "I'm sorry, Mel, I can't. I can't..."

"It's all right, I'll help you, my love," she

murmured between kisses. Each sweet touch of her lips brought him a breath of the warmth he remembered, buoying his spirits a little. "We need…Sptlk!"

The imp appeared, perched on top of the towel rail. An ideal vantage point to see both them and their reflections in the bathroom mirror, Luce realised, wondering if Sptlk had been watching them. The imp flashed his teeth in a wicked grin as he glanced at Luce, before giving Mel his full attention. "Respect, Lady. Respond to summons." He lifted a towel from the rail and bowed as he offered it to Mel.

Luce wrenched at the taps to turn the water off and grabbed a towel to dry himself. It was one thing for the imp to watch him giving pleasure to Mel, but it was another entirely to see him at his most vulnerable. He hoped Mel knew what she was doing, bringing the imp leader into their private business. Sptlk enjoyed causing trouble far too much for Luce's liking.

Mel wrapped her towel around her torso, tucking a corner in so that it hugged her like a strapless dress. "Sptlk, I want you to let Luce see through illusions like I can."

"But Lady…"

The imp hadn't mentioned payment, Luce realised. "Mel, he didn't say what he expects in return. They never do favours for free."

"Unthinkable disrespect, asking Lady for payment. Honoured to serve. Lord offers Lady deep disrespect. Must pay!" The imp's soul-voice sounded like a snarl in Luce's head – the first time he'd ever heard one of them angry.

"I have plenty of respect for Mel," Luce protested. "You never do anything for me without payment, so I thought…"

"Lord far beneath Lady. Never be her equal." The imp flooded Luce's mind with intimate images of himself and Mel, in sexual situations Luce wouldn't have dared to ask her about. "Has Lord repaid Lady for disrespect in Hell?"

Luce wished he could lie. Instead, he stomped out of the bathroom. He glanced over his shoulder as he reached the couch and was incensed to find that both Mel and the imp had followed him. The explicit images the imp projected grew even more imaginative.

Mel's gentle laughter surprised them both.

"Oh, that's sweet! You asked Sptlk to do something that contradicted my order and the payment he asked for the service was in very personal services to me? Luce, you should have said. And I thought all the offers of sex were just your rampant libido…"

Sptlk sniggered as Luce forced his mind to go blank.

"Sptlk, I need him to be able to see with no illusions at all. Remove them, please," Mel finished.

"As Lady wishes." The imp bowed and Mel's body dissolved into dust, leaving just a glittering cloud where Mel had been standing, only a moment before.

"Mel!" Luce choked out. His legs felt heavy and he fell to his knees, bowing so low his forehead touched the floorboards.

Five

A cold breeze wafted across Luce's bare arse before he heard the front door click closed. Oh Hell. Of all the times for some random visitor to wander into his house, they had to pick right now, while he was arse-up on the floor in the most submissive pose he'd ever held. Luce longed to get up, but he couldn't seem to make his body cooperate. He couldn't even raise his head to peer into the dust that occupied the space where Mel's body should be standing.

For humiliating him like this, Luce swore the imp would pay.

"Pay Lady in service," the imp's soul-voice said in his head. "Respect owed. No humiliation in offering respect. Angel should bow. Owes Lady greater debt than Lord." Sptlk seemed to hesitate. "Lord can return illusions with blink. Lady knows."

Shoes clomped across the floorboards. "Well, that's a sight to see when you walk in the door. Your taste has definitely improved since that demon I found in your house. That's one damn fine arse. I must say I approve, Mel."

"Please get up," Mel whispered.

She was still there, somehow. Or perhaps the dust was her, Luce decided, remembering how her body had disappeared outside the gates to Hell. The imp was right. He lost no face in prostrating himself before her – she was Lady Muriel, after all. No other angel on Earth stood higher than her – not even the one admiring his arse.

Luce lifted his head to squint into the glowing cloud. He saw Mel's true self now –

glittering gold outlined the feminine form he knew and loved. And she'd asked him to stand. Luce rose smoothly to his feet. "Thanks for the compliment. Of course Mel has impeccable taste. I sculpted this body for her pleasure." He cupped her face in his hands and kissed her until she gently disengaged from him.

"Luce. Please go put some pants on," she said.

Luce winked at Raphael. "As Lady Muriel commands." He blew Raphael a kiss. "Can't have you staring at my sexy arse all night." A glance at Mel told him she approved, though she was trying to smother a laugh with her hands. Still grinning, he marched off to find the promised pants.

Six

Luce dug out some casual pants that he knew showed his arse to the best advantage, then decided he'd best wear underwear, too. He selected some red silk boxers. He'd noticed the way Mel liked to stroke silk as much as skin and, if he had his way, once they'd evicted the interfering angel there'd be a lot of stroking going on.

"Cannot give Lady her desires," Sptlk said mournfully.

Luce's shock quickly turned to anger. "I will

give her anything and everything she desires. No matter what it takes. She deserves no less." He remembered the forced obeisance that had pinned his body to the floor. "What did you do to me in there? You made me look like a submissive slave!"

"Lady's orders. Remove illusions. See Lady as she truly is." The imp's eyes glittered with malice. "Remove all illusions. Illusion of self-worth, self-respect, arrogance, belief Lord is Lady's equal. Lady deserves more respect. Satisfaction to see Lord give."

Mel hadn't asked for it. The imp had obeyed her order to the letter, adding a broader meaning for his own reasons. Mel didn't want him bowing and scraping around her, Luce knew. Even the show of respect from the angels outside Heaven's gates had unsettled her. "I know I'm not good enough for her. I'm working on it. But she never asked me to be her equal. So what in Hell does she want that you think I can't give her?"

The imp settled onto the pillows, looking depressed. "Lady lacks strength and angels continue to sap it." The image was replaced with a blurry picture of Mel and Raphael, conversing quietly in the lounge. Mel's glowing soul seemed to dim. Even as he watched, glittering motes winked out.

Luce zipped up his pants. Without wasting time on a belt, he strode back to Mel.

"My sources say she's been spotted in Egypt. Some say in Cairo, while others say she frequents the ruins. There's talk that she's looking for the entrance to the old Underworld. The one before..." Raphael stopped abruptly to glare at Luce.

From warm glow to sparkling stars, Mel's soul had taken on a ragged appearance in Raphael's presence. She patted the seat cushion beside her, inviting Luce to sit down. "Raphael was just telling me that Persi might be in Egypt, but she's shying away from any angel who approaches her." She sighed. "I wish I knew what's troubling her."

Luce plonked his backside on the couch, making sure to sit as close to Mel as possible. This seemed to irritate Raphael no end, so Luce stretched an arm around Mel's bare shoulders to enrage the angel further. It also gave him better access to try and heal her, or hold her together. "Me, probably. The little half-angel was so obsessed with me she chained herself to my bed and tried to keep me out of Heaven." Hoping Mel didn't notice, Luce directed a tiny stream of healing energy into her body from his palm.

"I'll have Gabi book your flights for tomorrow," Raphael said eagerly. "It shouldn't take you more than a couple of weeks to check Egypt for her. Maybe three or four weeks, if you have to comb the desert, and you can –"

Go somewhere else to exhaust her even more when she desperately needed a holiday? To Hell with that.

"No."

Both Mel and Raphael stared at Luce. Her expression wasn't hostile – it was one of wonder.

"Mel's just sorted out a huge political mess in Japan after scouring London for your lost nephilim, and she needs rest," he continued. "That's why she's here. And I'm damn well going to make sure she gets it. Searching the bloody desert isn't something she should be doing — it's grunt work. I wouldn't send anything above a junior demon for that, and it'll go faster if you have more searchers. Get your Grigori on it or I'll send some demons instead. I'm taking Mel on holiday so she doesn't have to deal with this sort of stupidity. You're supposed to be the director of an agency full of helpful angels. Find some damn helpful angels and stop bothering your boss!" Luce bared his teeth in a snarl.

Raphael cleared his throat, looking like more than his throat was irritated. "Mel, put a leash on your pet demon. This is angels' business and none of his concern."

Luce glanced at Mel. She smiled serenely back, but she didn't say a word. Was she waiting, or simply too tired to speak? Luce took her silence as permission. "The Hell it isn't. You dragged her and me into this because you lost one of your employees. Now we're both managing the HELL Corporation for you, while we attempt to do our normal jobs, too. It's a wonder Mel doesn't demote you to gate guard like that nuisance Michael. It beggars belief that she lets you stay in a position of authority when you're this useless. She's got way more patience than I'll ever have. Find that girl on your own. Mel's done enough. She needs to recharge and sending her on another wild goose chase is the last thing she needs." Luce saw a fleeting look of panic cross Raphael's face before it disappeared. "You're just trying to keep her away from me, aren't you? Fat chance. The only one I take orders from is Mel."

"She should have left you to rot in Hell," Raphael hissed.

Mel rose and Luce stood beside her, not willing to let go of the fragile angel. "Raphael, that's unacceptable, as you well know. Answer Luce, please. Have you sent your team of Grigori into Egypt to follow up this lead?"

"No."

She bowed her head. "Then do so, please. Helping Luce out of Hell took quite a toll on me, at a time when I had little strength to spare. Luce is right that I need time to recuperate. We will continue to help with the HELL Corporation, but I leave the search for Persi in your capable hands. Bring her to me as soon as you find her and make sure every angel knows that I want her found. Perhaps she'll hear the gossip and come to me of her own volition."

Raphael oozed relief. "Sure. I'll give you daily updates on their progress and –"

"No," Mel said softly. "I only want to know if you find her. Contact me through Luce, for he'll know where I am. Raphael, give me your hand." Luce felt a burning flare of jealousy as Mel's fingers wrapped around the archangel's much larger ones.

Raphael's eyes widened in shock and further into horror. Luce hid a smile as the archangel fell to his knees. "Mel, I'm so sorry. I had no idea. Let me call Patrick. Koyane. Anyone. Someone to watch over you while you're this weak."

She released his hand and sank onto the sofa, breaking the healing contact between herself and Luce. "No. Luce is doing an admirable job so far and I like his recovery plan, too. He'll take good care of me."

Raphael's gaze wove uncertainly between Mel and Luce. "You can't. Please, Mel. I should never have asked for your help against the HELL Corporation. If I hadn't, you'd be safe and well and he wouldn't know where you are."

Mel lifted her chin, her eyes blazing. "You asked for my help and my condition was that I would assist in my own way. Forgive me if my plans are more far-reaching than yours, changing as circumstances require. My projects are completed to my specifications, not yours. And if Luce wishes, he will play a significant part in them."

"You can't trust him. No matter what you think he's become, he's still…"

"Lucifer, light of the morning, Lord of Hell and my love," Mel said steadily. "As you are Raphael of the Hashmallim and my trusted lieutenant. And you will understand one another. I want you both to shake hands." Her voice was deadly quiet. "Now."

Luce extended his hand to the angel, keeping his face carefully blank. "I will protect her at all costs. Even from you and the rest of her own kind."

Raphael gripped Luce's had firmly. "Harm

her and I'll lead all the forces of Heaven against you. Then we'll see the true colour of your blood."

"I would spill every drop for her." Luce found that if he concentrated, he could faintly sense the angel's soul and the turbulent emotions churning through it. The fierce protectiveness for Mel, anger and frustration, strong attraction he was trying to resist for…Luce? Luce fought to maintain his composure as he dug deeper into the angel's psyche. Desire and disgust, and fear for… "Michael. Mel, did you know this dick's Michael's boyfriend? That explains a lot."

Raphael reddened and yanked his hand away. "Everyone knows demons lie."

Luce winked. "Ah, but I'm not a demon any more, and angels don't lie. That means you can't lie, either. Does Mel know you're banging Michael?"

"Luce, Michael and Raphael have been close friends for a very long time. Given their natural inclinations, it seemed inevitable that their friendship would blossom into more. I wish you both well of each other, Raphael. Tell my brother the same, the next time you see him."

Now it was Luce's turn to look from Mel to Raphael and back again. Mel's serenity contrasted with Raphael's acute embarrassment. For all that Mel had known, Raphael hadn't told her a thing.

The angel seemed lost for words. Finally, he said, "If you need me for anything, let me know."

Mel leaned forward. "Find Persi. She needs your help more than I do."

Raphael nodded and hurried out. He almost collided with the waiter wheeling their order for room service, but he dodged around the man and continued on his way.

Seven

"Dinner!" Luce exclaimed. He heard Mel's footsteps fading away behind him – going to get dressed, he guessed. Ushering the waiter into the house, he led the way to the dining table. The man identified which covered dish was which, told Luce to leave the trolley and dishes outside when he was done and assured him one of the restaurant staff would collect them later tonight or early in the morning.

Luce locked the door behind the man and returned to the table. "Oh my God."

Mel blushed, glancing down at her white nightdress. It was just translucent enough to show she wore nothing underneath the silky fabric clinging to her curves, while covering all of the essentials. "I figured this would be more appropriate than day clothes, seeing as I intend to go to bed right after we're done with dinner. I hope you don't mind."

"Not at all. I think that's a brilliant plan. Dinner, then bed," Luce blurted out. If he wasn't absolutely starving, he'd happily skip dinner and take her straight to bed now.

Mel eyed the trolley. "So, what did you order for dinner?"

Luce pulled out a chair and waved extravagantly. "Take a seat, my lady, and let me serve you."

She laughed softly and sat. After a moment's confusion, Luce worked out which were the entrées and set Mel's before her. He poured her wine, too, before he sat across from her with his oysters and wine. He lifted the cover from her plate with a flourish. "Stuffed mushrooms. You like them, don't you?"

Mel nodded. "Much better than oysters."

He grinned as he lifted a shell to his lips. "Hey, I'm eating these at your command. I even ordered an extra dozen in case you wanted to share."

She swallowed her mouthful of mushroom. "Luce, I don't need shellfish to stimulate my desire. But you'll need every one of them for what I have in mind." Wickedly angelic eyes regarded him over her wineglass as she sipped.

Luce choked.

"Are you all right, my love?"

He coughed out some sort of reply that included the word 'fine' and headed for the kitchen for a big drink to wash down the troublesome oyster. Did she mean what he thought she did? All those times she'd turned him down…was it because his performance wasn't up to par? Was that why she was always so quiet and calm when he…when they…oh God. Loss of illusions…that damn imp. When he'd managed to get a hold of himself, he returned to find Mel had finished her mushrooms.

"Are you sure you're all right?" Mel asked, her worried eyes reading his very soul.

"No. I'm not, am I? I'm not good enough for you. After seeing your other men – Patrick and that Japanese one, Koyane – you started thinking about how perfect they are and how I'll never be an angel like that. Never was, never will be. And if you feel I need aphrodisiac food to be able to satisfy you…should I be buying that Viagra stuff next? Horny goat weed or whatever herbal supplements the human health food shops are peddling? I'll never be good enough for you, will I, Mel?"

Her horror said more than any words could. Luce knew he was right.

"I should serve your next course. At least I can manage that."

"Luce…"

He held up his hand to stop her. "You don't need to try and make me feel better. I know what I am. And your dinner will get cold while you slap a band-aid on my bruised ego."

Shoving his untouched oysters onto the trolley, Luce passed out the main course plates – some sort of creamy pasta with little prawns. Shrimp? Whatever they called those things. He poured more wine and shovelled forkfuls of food into his mouth so he wouldn't have to say anything else. He scraped the last shrimp through a drift of sauce and heard the clink and clatter of cutlery hitting the floor. He glanced up to see Mel swaying in her seat.

Luce rounded the table in two strides, grabbing her before her face landed in her half-eaten meal.

"I'm sorry," Mel mumbled with her eyes closed. "I can't seem to stay awake. So…tired. Didn't sleep enough on the plane and hardly at all in Japan."

"So go to bed then," Luce replied. She was probably up all night with that angel Koyane and maybe even the siren, too. The girl had been eyeing Mel with unconcealed lust since the moment they met.

"You've gone to so much trouble. I want to have dinner with you. I missed you." She levered her eyes open with considerable effort. "I missed you, Luce." The dark circles beneath her eyes were more noticeable now and she felt unusually heavy as she leaned against him, as if exhaustion had sapped even her will to sit up.

Luce swept her up in his arms. Now he could feel how tired she was — the heaviness in every limb and the cloying fog in her mind. "Bed or dinner?" he asked.

"I…" she began, then sighed, resting her head against his shoulder.

Her body needed both energy and sleep to repair, and she had said she wanted dinner. Luce dropped into her chair, hearing the timber creak beneath him at their combined weight. He hooked his leg around the chair beside him and pulled it out from under the table, then laid Mel's legs across it. Her head still rested against his shoulder, but he'd freed up his left arm to reach for his fork. He loaded it with a piece of Mel's filled pasta and lifted it to her lips. "Dinner, Melody?"

Gratitude warmed her half-closed eyes. "Thank you." Her sweet lips parted to permit the pasta inside and he felt the gentle jar of her teeth on the fork as her tongue swept the morsel deeper into her mouth. Reluctantly, Luce withdrew the fork, noticing a slight smear of sauce on her lips. The tip of her tongue took care of it before he could surrender to the desire to kiss her. She lifted her chin a touch as she swallowed, enticing Luce's attention to the silky skin of her throat and the smooth curve down to the swell of her breasts beneath the filmy white nightdress. His pants grew uncomfortably tight, but he forced himself to dip the fork into Mel's meal again.

Slowly he fed her, one bite at a time. Even the simple act of chewing and swallowing seemed a struggle for her. Unobtrusively, Luce stretched his soul out to touch hers once more, letting a trickle of healing flow between them. When she didn't react, he increased the intensity, praying she wouldn't stop him this time.

To cover his distraction, Luce trawled the tines of his fork through the thick sauce, looking for any pasta pieces he'd missed. Instead, he snagged a shrimp.

"Last one, Mel," he coaxed. "After this, it's dessert."

This time, she didn't open her mouth. Luce glanced down and realised her eyes were shut just as tight as her lips. He popped the prawn in his own mouth and let the fork clatter onto her plate. A deft swipe of the napkin removed the last traces of sauce. He debated whether to try and wake her or find somewhere more comfortable for her to sleep. Mel sighed and turned her face into his shoulder, a smile lifting her lips as her cheek rubbed against his skin.

To Hell with dessert. He was taking Mel to bed now before he burst through the zip of his pants. And nothing was sweeter than his angel.

Eight

Luce woke to loud banging on his front door. He heaved himself out of bed and glanced down in wonder as he realised he'd slept in not just his underwear, but his pants. That had to be a first. He clearly recalled carrying Mel to bed, then stretching out beside her for just a moment to finish healing her, but his memories were pretty vague after that.

His pants were just as tight as last night — maybe more so, he decided, adjusting himself. Was it worth waking Mel to ask her if she wanted to make use of his morning glory?

The banging sounded again, louder and more impatient than before.

He stumbled into the dining room and surveyed the dirty plates still on the table. He must've fallen asleep alongside Mel. A tinkling sound down near his foot caught his attention and Luce reached down to pick up the fork Mel had dropped.

The assault on his front door shook it in its frame. Was there a demon on the other side? Luce wondered. If there was, he'd tell them to go straight to Hell. He wasn't coming in to work today. He threw the door open to find himself facing an angry woman in chef's whites.

"The waitstaff have been up here twice and both times they've come back empty-handed. Neither of them wanted to knock on the door after what happened last time. We only do room service to the apartments if you return the dishes and there's only the one trolley. The head chef said you wanted breakfast room service, but we haven't received your order and I'm not cooking it until you return all the restaurant property, anyway." She plucked the fork from Luce's fingers. "Where's the rest of it?"

Luce left the door open and led the way to the dining room.

The woman stuck her hands on her hips and surveyed the mess. "So you had a woman over, seduced her with wine and good food, then talked her into your bed –" She lifted the lid on one of the covered dessert plates. The multicoloured, creamy creation had now congealed into an unappetising, pinkish brown puddle. "– and forgot about dessert. That must have been one hot night."

Luce summoned a grin. He couldn't lie, but he knew the right sexy smile could tell a tale all on its own.

"What was dessert?" Mel's voice startled him. She stood in the doorway, wearing one of those Japanese dressing-gown dresses over her nightgown. The golden bamboo patterned across the white fabric was the precise shade of her hair. "I'm sorry, Luce. Between the flight from Japan and not feeling well, I fell asleep and missed the best part of the evening." Her smile set Luce's heart aglow. "Thank you for taking such good care of me."

The chef snorted. "This one doesn't do anything for a woman without an ulterior motive. Do not trust a word he says — he'll seduce you into his bed and throw you out in the morning, if he remembers you're there. Ask him to tell you about the last time he didn't return his room service trolley. That wasn't the only thing he forgot. He left some poor girl handcuffed hand and foot to his bed. When I found her, the poor thing was naked and in tears, bleeding from trying to get out of the restraints. I don't know what would have happened to her if I hadn't come along. I had to get some pliers and a set of boltcutters from the caretaker to free her because he'd forgotten to leave her the keys to her metal handcuffs, too." She glared at Luce. "The only reason I didn't call the police is because she begged me not to."

Luce snorted. "So that's how she got free. She hid the keys, not me. One set up each hole. I wasn't sticking my fingers up her to get them out. Serves her right. She put them on."

"Don't trust him," the woman insisted. "He'll be just as callous when he's done with you. Get out while you still have your self-respect."

"That must have been the night you came to my place, running through the rain as if all the hounds of Hell were after you. I bet she didn't want the police involved. Persi can be frighteningly persistent when she develops an obsession for someone, like she did for you." Mel tucked herself into Luce's side and kissed his cheek. She turned her eyes on the chef. "Thank you for rescuing my cousin from her predicament, and for saving Luce from having to deal with her when he got home. I heard you mention breakfast?"

"I mentioned it, but according to restaurant policy, he'll be cooking it for you, not me," the woman said, piling the dirty plates onto the trolley.

Luce watched in fascination as Mel stepped forward and rested her hand on the woman's wrist. The chef's mesmerised eyes met Mel's and didn't look away. "Perhaps you didn't hear me. The woman you found chained herself to a bed in her relentless pursuit of her boss and my partner. He deserted his own home to get away from her. I don't believe he'd have ordered dinner for the two of them – just himself – so if the meal was for two last time, she ordered it. Any inconvenience my cousin caused you is between your employer and Persephone, not Luce. This morning's misunderstanding is my fault. My flight arrived late yesterday and Luce ordered food to save me from cooking, given how weary I was." She laughed gently. "I'm sure your employer wouldn't want to alienate one of his best customers because that customer chose to place the health of his partner over some dirty dishes and the enjoyment of what I believe looks like some delicious dessert?" Mel sighed. "I wish I'd been well enough to eat it last night."

Luce wanted to applaud, but he didn't dare.

"We'll see," the woman responded grudgingly. She pulled her hand out from under Mel's and finished clearing the table.

"What would you like for breakfast?" Luce asked Mel, ignoring the other woman.

Mel smiled. "Actually, I don't think I'm ready to eat anything yet. I was just thirsty. I only got up to get a glass of water."

"Let me," he said, grabbing the jug of filtered water from the fridge. He presented a filled glass to her.

Mel's smile didn't fade as she sipped her way through Luce's offering, before setting the empty glass on the sink. "Thank you. I'm still a bit tired, so if you don't mind, I'd like to go back to bed for some more sleep."

"Of course." Luce's heart flipped as her light kiss tingled against his lips. He watched her careful steps back to their shared bedroom.

The door clicked closed behind the departing chef and Luce seriously considered following Mel back to bed. No, he decided. He had a holiday to plan.

He powered up his laptop and switched on the coffee machine. How did you plan a holiday from HELL with a perfect angel like Mel?

Like the honeymoon from Heaven. He grinned and started his search, slurping his espresso in bliss.

Nine

Ninety frustrating minutes later, Luce had managed to book exactly nothing. Not flights, accommodation…he couldn't even decide on a destination. Would Mel want beaches or snow or wilderness or city or…what?

He picked up the phone and prayed it was a good idea. He needed help, after all.

"Hello, Helpful Angels Agency," a professional, feminine voice bubbled. "How may I help you?"

Luce thanked Heaven and anyone else

who'd answered his prayer. "I'm hoping you can help. I intend to take my angel on a relaxing holiday and I'm looking for recommendations."

The girl cleared her throat. "Ah, I believe you might have the wrong impression. You see, this is an employment agency and not a travel agency. We provide expert staff to meet our clients' needs and…"

"And the expert assistance I need is advice on where to take an angel on holiday. From the HELL Corporation. One of your expert staff." Luce stressed the last two words, just in case she didn't get the message.

"Is this a joke? Or a threat?" The bubbles popped, baring steel. Luce recognised her voice now. "I hope you realise that threatening our staff contravenes several laws and violates your contract of service with us. What is your name…or the name of the staff member?"

Luce gritted his teeth. "My name is Luce Iblis and you sound like Gabrielle…D'Angelo, isn't it?"

"It sure is, and I'll be telling Raphael and every other angel I see today that you're threatening Mel. They'll carve you into little demon cubes and skewer you for your subordinates to barbeque in Hell before you can blink. Don't you even think of taking Mel anywhere."

He burst out laughing. "Your boss already knows – Mel told him herself last night. And he knows what the consequences will be if he tries to stop me again."

"Go to Hell," Gabrielle snapped and slammed the phone down.

Bloody unhelpful angel.

Luce noticed a text message from an unknown number, so he opened it.

Your cock is smaller than shrimp and your stamina is sucking.

Wrong number. Definitely. Luce deleted it.

Sighing, Luce grimaced and did what he always did when he needed a problem sorted.

"Good morning, Mr Iblis," Mephi answered on the second ring. Feminine and professional, but with bite from the beginning. At least she was honest.

"Hi, Mephi. As I mentioned yesterday, I won't be in for the better part of the next month as I take some overdue leave. Melody Angel, too. But I need your help."

"What with, Mr Iblis?"

"I don't know where to take her on holiday. I promised we'd go away somewhere but I don't know what she'd like and I can't ask her." Well, he could, but that would spoil the surprise and making her help him plan the whole thing was hardly him arranging a relaxing holiday for her.

"Mr Iblis, what does Miss Angel like?"

Luce racked his brain. "Macchiato. Fresh-brewed tea. Chocolate. Wine. Good food. Swans. Wild birds. Dolphins. Weather like we have here. Warm water she can swim in. Whiskey. Fishing. No, wait – not fishing. That wasn't her idea and he regretted it. Scented flowers. Caves, I think. Not too many people around. Fresh milk. Long walks through trees with wildlife. God, I don't know!"

"She told me once that she liked the hot springs in Japan. Perhaps –"

"NO!" Luce exploded. "She just got back

from there and the angel she was staying with had the hots for her. I'm not sharing her with anyone!"

Mephi cleared her throat. "In that case, perhaps a place with a spa. Most of the things you referred to are found here, in the south-west of this state. Perhaps you should be looking for secluded retreats here in the south-west? I've heard there's a new whisky distillery opening in Margaret River and they have some rather luxurious honeymoon-style accommodation in that area. The only other places with a similar climate would be California and Tuscany. I'd have to check if those have the sort of wilderness you want…"

"Margaret River? Where in Hell's that?"

"Three to four hours' drive south of your present location and close to the coast. If you leave now, you could be there in time for a late lunch, Mr Iblis."

And spend tonight in a honeymoon retreat with his precious angel? Heaven.

"Thanks, Mephi."

Silence, then a hesitant, "You're welcome, Mr Iblis. Please take good care of Miss Angel.

Yesterday, she looked…tired." Mel had even managed to melt her way into his PA's stone heart – no small feat, he knew.

"I will." Luce ended the call and tossed his phone on the table.

It beeped as he received another text message.

If woman come on your cock it is fake.

Luce snorted. Whoever these messages were meant for, they were definitely a complete loser in bed. He almost felt sorry for the bugger.

He started searching for accommodation in Margaret River with a spa. Just the thought of sharing the hot, bubbling water with Mel gave his fingers wings as they flew across the laptop keyboard.

Ten

Luce pushed his chair away from the table, feeling unusually proud of himself. He'd booked their accommodation, made some dinner reservations and even planned a few activities that Mel might like. All he had left to do was make sure they were both packed and head down there. Just the two of them in his car on the open road.

He slipped into the bedroom, laying his suitcase on the floor so he could start packing. Maybe he could open the curtains just a little to let some light in without waking Mel. He glanced at her and met her open eyes. "How are you feeling?" Luce perched on the edge of the bed.

Mel sat up. "Better." She reached for his hand and he clasped her warm fingers. "Being with you helps. You're good for me, Luce."

He laughed. He wasn't good for anyone – that he knew for certain. But he was trying. "I'm sure it's the other way 'round. Are you ready for the best holiday ever?"

"My first holiday ever," Mel confessed.

"Mine, too. But I don't need it anywhere near as much as you do. I swear I'll take care of you, Melody."

"I know you will and that's why I'm here. Not London, not Japan, not Heaven, but here with you." Mel's trusting smile lifted Luce's heart.

Before it crashed and burned. This time yesterday, he'd have believed he was the best one for her. He could do anything. Now, thanks to that damned imp, he wasn't even sure he could drive them to their destination without getting lost. Mel deserved better. He'd

BE better – but would he be good enough? Or would she leave him and head somewhere else, to hook up with other angels who knew her better than he did? Who could take care of her better than he could, in every way possible?

"I should pack," he said, striding into the walk-in wardrobe.

"And I should freshen up," Mel replied.

When he returned to the bedroom with an armful of clothes, the freshly-made bed was empty and he could hear the shower raining onto the tiles. He ached to join her in the bathroom, to feel the flow of hot water over their close-pressed bodies as he kissed her, as he caressed her…

No. Luce forced himself to fold clothes into his suitcase instead. No matter how much he wanted her, she was tired and needed rest. And he was afraid he wouldn't be good enough for her, a small voice in the back of his mind said. It sure as Hell wasn't his voice.

"Lord remain indebted for eternity," Sptlk sniggered, perching on the lid of Luce's suitcase. "Must repay Lady. Learn better." Luce caught a glimpse of the image of Mel's rapturous, flushed face before the imp brushed it away. "Give Lady joy. Debt repaid."

"Last night you said I couldn't fulfil Mel's desires. Now you say I can, but I have to learn how? Make up your damn mind and quit messing with Mel. She has enough trouble from her own kind. Reverse what you did yesterday and then leave. I don't want to see you in…the place where we're going." Luce glared at the imp.

Sptlk flashed his needle-like teeth in what Luce presumed was meant to be a smile. "Not without Lady's order. Must ask Lady."

Tell Mel his self-confidence, his prowess in bed, his pride, all of it…was just an illusion that the imp had stolen from him and now he wanted it back? When the only way he could learn to share their bond was without them? No way in Hell. He just had to learn faster. Once he'd mastered this soul communication thing, then he could tell her and ask for all that back. But not before.

Sptlk's smile widened as he observed Luce's dilemma. The calculating look in his eyes hardened. "No illusions, then.

Leave…perhaps. What price Lord pay for privacy?"

Luce's mind went blank. "I don't know. Everything I do right now is for Mel. Only Mel." He felt incredibly weary – like Mel seemed to be. "You know, to Hell with it. Watch if you want to. Laugh and get off and share me as one big joke with all your mates. I wouldn't know the first thing about taking care of a burned-out angel, let alone one as precious as Mel, but I'm damn well going to try to do the best I can for her. I won't be the Lord of Hell for much longer. As soon as Mel finds something better for me to do, you'll get someone else to make bargains with. Maybe someone who wants to seduce more people than I could. Hell, maybe even someone with more stamina." He wrenched open his sock drawer and threw pairs into the suitcase.

One almost hit Sptlk, but he stepped aside just in time. "Will leave. Will not appear while Lady…recovers. Will check. Lord must restore Lady. Lady…precious indeed."

"You're saying you'll leave us alone, provided I help Mel?" Luce didn't believe it.

Sptlk nodded sharply. "Restoration gift to Lady. Lady…is loved." The imp vanished.

Bloody cryptic creature. What in Hell did it mean? He was in love with Mel, too? Wasn't Sptlk a demon, like he used to be? How in Hell could it love anyone?

Luce dumped a pile of underwear on top of the socks and savagely zipped the suitcase closed. At least he wouldn't have any imps watching over his shoulder as he struggled to take care of Mel. What had he gotten himself in for? The Lord of Hell was best at corrupting souls, not restoring them. He hadn't a hope in Hell of succeeding.

Eleven

Perfection herself appeared in the bedroom. Beauty personified. Creamy-gold curves like the most heavenly body Luce had ever seen, lit by the same pearly glow as Heaven's gates. He'd never be able to look at another woman again without comparing her to this paragon no one could match.

Mel's laughter bubbled infectiously. "Luce, you're staring at me as if you've never seen a naked woman before, and I know that's not true. Not to mention how well you know this body." Her hands cupped her breasts and Luce's breath caught in his throat.

He wasn't worthy to touch her – probably not even to look at her. Every inch of her was flawless, from the damp strands of hair that hung over unfathomably deep, grey eyes to her perfectly formed, pink toes. He loved her, but he'd never seen her look like this before. Had she somehow recovered as she slept and this was the result? He was dying to touch her, to see if the Mel he was seeing was real or just an illusion.

Wait. Illusion…in the absence of illusions, this was Mel in her true form. The imperfections he'd always seen were the illusion. If he squinted, he could even see the faint blur of her wings, but he didn't want to, because the white feathers would obscure the vision before him.

The bloody imp knew it. He could take the illusions and all his insecurities would vanish…but he'd never see Mel like this. Or he could have his perfect angel and not have the guts to touch her, let alone anything else.

"Luce." Damn, she looked like she'd been

calling him for a while. Mel smiled when he finally met her eyes. "I asked if you were going to tell me where we're going, or is it a surprise?"

"I want to surprise you," he replied.

How had he missed her getting dressed? Her perfect breasts were now hidden inside a t-shirt that stretched over what looked like a lace-edged bra, if he recognised the outline right. And those spectacular legs were encased in thick denim as she buttoned her jeans.

"But how will I know what to pack? Will I need ski clothes, wet weather gear, my swimsuit…"

"I could pack for you," he said eagerly. He'd pack her skimpiest underwear and sexiest clothing, so he could admire her assets every waking moment.

Mel blushed as if she was reading his thoughts. Uneasily, Luce wondered if she was. "No, Luce, I should do that."

Ah, Hell. There went the idea of a complete surprise. "Pack…for weather like here." When she opened her mouth to ask something else, he added, "Pack clothes as if I were taking you to some luxury hotel here in Perth for the next month, and we'd walk through Kings Park every day. I'm not, but —" he winked "— that's all you'll get out of me until we arrive at our destination."

Mel nodded slowly. "All right. You're being awfully mysterious, my love, but I trust you." A peculiar sound, like a muffled flock of lorikeets, squeaked from her mid-section. "Oh, um…what did you say was for breakfast?"

Breakfast? Hell, he'd completely forgotten. "I'll go out and get some muffins or something while you pack," Luce said and hurried out. He opened the front door and stubbed his toes on the big basket right outside. He tore off the piece of paper wrapped around the handle and tried to make sense of the scrawl. "Picnic brunch for two," he read, skimming over the numbers and the restaurant letterhead until he reached the words at the bottom. "Get well soon."

Snorting, he hefted the basket inside and set it on the dining table. It looked like Mel had made an impression on someone — but the unforgiving chef had still made her point in giving them no trolley, or crockery or cutlery to return, he found as he started pulling things out of the basket. He headed into the kitchen for the necessary items.

Luce returned to the dining room just in time to see Mel sink her teeth into an almond croissant. She swallowed what was evidently a delicious mouthful, judging by her expression, before she opened her eyes.

"Fresh croissants. You're wonderful, Luce." She kissed his cheek and dusted off the icing sugar she'd left behind.

He grinned. "Not yet. I still have to make you a coffee and I know exactly how you like it."

Twelve

As Luce accelerated past the airport off-ramps, Mel folded her arms. "I guess I don't need my passport, then."

Luce paused to swear under his breath at the stupid human drivers who didn't understand how to merge into freeway traffic before he replied, "Was that what you wanted? I can turn us around and fly you anywhere in the world if you want. Just say the word, Mel." They weren't even there yet and he'd messed up already.

Mel laughed lightly. "No, I trust that whatever you have in mind will be wonderful. I just had you pegged as the billionaire with a private island sort of holiday planner. And you did mention a luxury hotel."

"We could be driving to where the luxury ship's moored that will take us to a private island…" Luce began.

"We could," Mel agreed. Her enigmatic smile drove all thoughts of continuing the conversation out of Luce's head, so he concentrated on overtaking the tiny hatchback whose owner seemed to have misread the speed limit as seventy instead of a hundred.

Her expression didn't change as they sped south, though her eyes took in everything outside the car. After a couple of hours, the radio dissolved into static, so he switched it off. Mel said nothing, if she even noticed. She seemed too busy looking at the endless repetition of paddocks and trees outside her window.

By the time they hit Bussell Highway, Luce was dying to know what Mel was thinking. He could see the building excitement in her eyes and he desperately prayed he'd made the right decision. She looked startled when he turned onto a road between two paddocks, but still she didn't say anything. Signs pointed to the chocolate company and Luce slowed down, but he didn't stop until he'd passed it, when the road ended and he needed to turn. He grinned when Mel stared at him.

"We can go there first thing tomorrow. I want to show you where we'll be staying first. Don't worry, I know how much you love chocolate and I wouldn't deny you the pleasure." He chuckled.

Mel pressed her lips together and maintained her silence, but her smile returned, along with a faint blush.

A few minutes later, he turned again and the tyres grated across gravel as he negotiated the narrow track that led into the bush. The sign said it was the right place, but it didn't look like much. Maybe he should have booked that luxury hotel in the middle of town, but he wanted privacy with Mel. If they got a poky hotel room, however luxurious, it would be smaller and closer to people than in his penthouse. They might as well have stayed home.

They bumped down the road until they reached a modern concrete building that was the same shade of orange as the gravel. Luce parked and strode around the car to open Mel's door for her before offering a hand to help her out.

"Thank you," she said as she took his hand. She laced her fingers through his as she stood beside him. "Are we going in?"

Luce nodded and pushed open the glass door.

He heard Mel take a deep breath as she stepped inside. "Mmm, sugar, red wine and…ooh, nougat. What are we here for?"

"All of it, if you want," Luce replied. Together, they approached the counter.

Two couples were tasting wine as a man wearing casual clothes and a gardening tool-belt – complete with secateurs – leaned on the counter and offered them more wine. "Be right with you," he told Luce before turning his attention back to the others.

Ten minutes later, the couples staggered to

their cars under the weight of their boxes of wine and Luce stepped up to the counter.

"What would you like to taste first?" the man asked, setting two clean glasses on the counter.

Melody's lips. The thought hit Luce out of the blue and he struggled not to blurt it out.

"What do you recommend?" Mel asked, wearing her sweetest smile.

The man poured and described the wines, one by one, from the fresh-flavoured white through the strong reds. By the time they reached the chili wine that Luce almost choked on, he'd lost the plot somewhere between the tannins, oaks and berries.

"What do you call this?" Luce asked hoarsely, pointing at the chili one.

"That's part of our Lost Plot range," the man said.

Mel laughed. "I can see why. I'd like to buy some. Is that all right, Luce?"

Since when did she need his permission for anything? "Buy as much as you like, Mel. If it doesn't fit in the car or we don't drink it while we're here, we'll ship it home. We'll be here a month – you can come back down here whenever you like."

The man seemed to understand something he hadn't before. "Are you Mr Iblis?"

Luce nodded. "I'm Luce Iblis. I've booked your honeymoon apartment."

It was Mel's turn to choke.

Luce slipped an arm around her waist. "If you don't like it, we'll go somewhere else. Anywhere you want, I promise."

The man cleared his throat. "There aren't any refunds if you cancel within four weeks of your stay." He looked smug. "But once they've seen it, no one's ever said they don't like it."

Luce shrugged. "Time to show us, then. Where's this secluded retreat?"

The man laughed and pointed. "Upstairs."

He led the way outside and up the stairs that Luce had thought led to a rooftop deck. He was half right – the loft apartment did have veranda decking, with French doors opening out onto the balcony, beside a wrought iron table and chairs. The man handed the key to Mel and invited her to unlock the door.

She looked like she thought it was a joke,

but she turned the key and pushed the door open. Luce stepped inside right behind her, so he heard her first gasp. Mel spun on the spot and threw her arms around his neck. "You're wonderful, Luce. This place is perfect." She followed this up with a wonderful, perfect kiss that Luce personally thought was much better than the luxury, open plan apartment with views across the winery. Even with the spa big enough for both of them.

The man behind them said, "I guess I'll leave you two to it. I'm Greg – I own the place. If you need anything, just drop into the tasting room downstairs between ten and five. After five, you'll have the whole place to yourself, but when the tasting room's open…well, you might want to keep the windows closed if you don't want anyone knowing what you're doing." Greg's eyebrows seemed to say he knew what they'd be doing, all the same.

"Thank you." Mel beamed at him and he left.

Luce wrapped his arms tightly around her. "I wanted something secluded so you could relax properly without too many people around. So we could… I looked for retreats and honeymoon accommodation because I figured they'd give us privacy. This is our first holiday and I don't want to share it with a bunch of humans. Just you."

Mel shook her head gently. "It doesn't matter where we are. You could have put us up in a dorm at the backpackers hostel in town. As long as we're together, it will still be a wonderful holiday. But this…this…" She waved at the apartment. "You couldn't take better care of me if you tried, Luce. Like I said, it's perfect."

Luce grinned. "I'll go get our bags then, shall I? While you work out the most comfortable place to sit and admire the view."

Thirteen

"Let's go. I've made dinner reservations and this restaurant comes highly recommended." Luce grabbed his phone and noticed the message light was blinking. Automatically, he checked it.

Your cock is too small to fuck.

Luce tried not to snort. Yep, another wrong message to delete. He wondered what the sender would say if she (he?) knew that most of Luce's random text messages were the opposite – past bed partners telling him how they couldn't forget him, his body, his prowess or a combination of all three and how much they wanted all three again. He hoped Mel didn't see any of them – the encounters had all been a long time ago, but he was pretty unforgettable.

If he got any more from this person who was fixated on diminutive dicks, he was going to respond by unzipping his pants, taking a picture and sending evidence to the phantom message-sender that they had the wrong man. But right now, dinner with Mel was more important. Well, unless she wanted to help him take the photo…

"What are you thinking about?" Mel's arms slid around him. "I know that cheeky grin. It usually means you have something fun planned that you're waiting to surprise me with. Please tell me it's not a live seafood restaurant. Keiko tried to drag me to one of those in Japan, but Koyane managed to talk her out of it. If someone sets a live octopus in front of me again, it'll put me off my dinner."

Luce laughed. "I'd like to make love to you so thoroughly it'd feel like you had a live octopus, with eight arms instead of two. But taking care of you means dinner first, so I'll keep my tentacles in my pants for now." No matter how hard it was to restrain himself. "This restaurant is part wine bar, so I hope you're willing to indulge in a drink or three with your dinner."

"Only if you join me," she responded.

He grinned. "I'll do my best, but it's in town, so I'll be driving. I can't drink too much."

The restaurant turned out to be in the next town, almost half an hour's drive south. Luce parallel-parked his car smoothly right outside the restaurant door and, moments later, found himself seated comfortably beside Mel in a tiny, curved booth for two.

"You look like a honeymoon couple, and that's our booth for honeymooners," the hostess told them. "Where are you staying?"

Mel's blush was visible even in the dimly lit restaurant. "In a loft apartment on top of a winery, just outside of Cowaramup."

The woman burst out laughing. "Yep, I knew it. Honeymooners for sure." She lowered her voice. "Seeing as it's your first night here, I'll arrange a free cocktail for you. What would you like?"

Luce opened his mouth to say they hadn't had time to read the drinks menu yet, but Mel was faster. "I'd like a Dark n' Stormy, please, but not yet. With dessert."

The woman shot a knowing glance at Luce and winked. "Will do. Now, shall I leave you two to it for a few minutes? I'll be back in a moment to take the rest of your order."

With Mel cuddled up to his side, Luce found it hard to focus on the menu. There weren't any oysters, but he thought he'd seen some prawns. Like he'd shared with Mel last night, holding her in his arms and watching each morsel slip between her lips as he wished it was his tongue. Or maybe… Tiger prawns. There they were. And burgers. Layers lying one on top of the other like he'd like to be right now…

"Are you ready to order?" The hostess had returned and she looked expectant.

Luce floundered. A slight nod from Mel told him she was, but he had no idea. "How about you order for me?" he suggested.

The hostess' mouth dropped open.

"If you like, my love," Mel responded. She lifted her gaze to smile squarely at their server. "For entrée, Luce will have the angel hair pasta with crab, while I'll have the prawn croquettes. Mains…mm, I think the seared duck breast for both of us with a serve of seasonal vegetables on the side. I have no idea if I'll even want dessert – especially with that tempting cocktail. Can we order dessert after dinner if that's what we'd like?"

The server nodded quickly, then checked her order. "Ah…any other drinks?"

"Oh! Of course." Mel promptly rattled off the list of wines she wanted served – before dinner and with each course. Even Luce was impressed.

The bemused hostess wandered off with her order pad and Mel whispered, "Is that all right? We can change it, if you want."

Luce laughed. "I'm sure everything will be fine. You know my tastes better than anyone and I'll probably be so busy focussing on you I won't taste a bite of my food, anyway. Tonight, I'll finally have you all to myself again. No neighbours, well-meaning friends or staff. Just us." He leaned in to kiss her and whispered, "I promise I'll be slow and gentle tonight. Anything you want from me – just name it and it's yours." He illustrated his point with a soft, drawn-out kiss.

The clink of glass broke their embrace, as Mel turned to smile at the server for the glasses of sparkling white wine. Luce grabbed a glass and raised it. "To your health," he said.

Mel silently touched her glass to his, seconding his toast, before slowly sipping the contents. Her sweet smile made Luce take a deep draught of his own drink. Light and fizzy and fruity.

Food followed drink and then more of both. Luce ate, drank and stared at Mel, content for the first time he could remember. Somewhere in the back of his mind were the worries that Mel would leave him, that he wasn't good enough for her, and all the other simmering insecurities that wouldn't go away, but none of those mattered right now. The warmth in her eyes said she loved him.

"Can I get you the dessert menu?" the hostess asked, startling Luce out of his blissful bubble. She took their empty plates and Luce couldn't recall what had been served on it.

He picked something random from the menu and Mel ordered cheese. When their order came, the server placed a glass of what looked like cola or ginger beer in front of Mel. The cheese platter sat in the middle of the table and a dish was set carefully between Mel and Luce. Between the two spoons rose a small scarp of ice cream, dusted with green powder that resembled grass.

"What's that?" Luce asked, eyeing both Mel's drink and the ice cream.

"This is my cocktail and that is your ice cream with pistachio," Mel replied. "Would you like to taste it?" She held out the glass.

Luce took a deep sniff. The raw scent of rum seared his nostrils and he hurriedly gave the drink back. "No. But I want to share this ice cream with you." He skimmed a spoon through it, holding it up for Mel.

She took it from him, smiling as she swallowed. "Ooh, that's lovely. Salty and sweet, with a slightly gritty texture from the nuts. You're going to make me wish I'd ordered that instead of the cheese. Make sure you have some, too."

"Half is yours," Luce insisted, nudging the second spoon.

For the first time in his life, he shared a dessert – and who better to share it with than the sweetest angel he'd ever known?

Fourteen

Mel's relaxed smile as they made their way back to the car set Luce's heart soaring. Her slight tipsiness gave him the perfect excuse to keep his arm around her and the warmth of her along his side was Heaven in the cold night air.

He helped her into her seat and climbed behind the steering wheel. The key had just touched the ignition when his phone rang.

Luce didn't recognise the number, but he answered it anyway. The caller's response was a string of feminine moans. Luce pulled the phone from his ear and squinted at the number again. The screen was filled with a pop-up message, asking if he wanted to turn his camera on for the video call. Hastily, he refused. The message vanished and revealed a dim, blurry picture that Luce couldn't discern.

The picture seemed to tilt, as if someone had moved the phone, and what looked like a man's wrinkled thumb came into view. The camera jiggled and shifted again and the picture became clearer. No, it wasn't a man's thumb…though the appendage definitely belonged to a man, and in the background was a naked woman, lying face down with her legs spread wide. The camera swooped in close to the woman's genitals as a male voice snapped something in a language Luce didn't understand.

Mel reached for the phone and muted the microphone. "He said that she is what you will never have, because she is his."

A ringed hand slapped the woman's rump, eliciting squeals from the woman.

The phone travelled over the woman's body

to her bound forearms, where it was presumably placed in her hands. When her blurry, flushed face came into view, Mel murmured, "That's Mrs Han and the voice sounds like Mr Han."

The man swatted her backside a few times and growled something.

"Tell him what you told me," Mel translated. She paused as Mrs Han squealed a string of syllables. "I am his and you will never...touch my body again." Her hesitation made Luce suspect that Mel was sanitising her translation. "Watch how a real man does it. Please, please make love to me, yes." Mel's calm delivery contrasted strongly with the impassioned cries of Mrs Han as Mr Han plunged enthusiastically into his willing wife.

"Yes, yes, more. Harder."

"Take it. Take it. You like that baby?"

"Yes, yes, oh yes."

A splatter of fluid landed on the camera lens, mercifully blurring the picture but doing nothing to muffle Mrs Han's rapturous screams. A few more growled words from Mr Han resulted in another string of breathless gibberish from Mrs Han.

Mel cleared her throat. "He said to tell you all of it. She said…ah, she loves her big Dong and she is his alone. You are smaller than her…little finger and…generally unskilled." Her blush was visible even in the dark car, but Luce's cheeks were on fire.

"She's asking for your response."

Luce stared desperately at Mel and the phone. "I don't speak Korean. I don't know what to say. What do you say to that?"

"May I?" Mel's finger hovered over the mute button. Luce nodded eagerly. Mel assumed a professional smile and unleashed a stream of fluent Korean in her perfectly modulated voice. She paused several times, as if waiting for a response from the panting couple, but continued when it appeared no response was forthcoming. To Luce's relief, she soon ended the call.

"What did you say?" he asked shakily, not sure he wanted to know.

Mel's eyes danced in the light of an oncoming car. "I congratulated them on reconciling their marital difficulties and told them that we were presently on extended leave, but if they required our diplomatic services, to contact Mephi at the HELL Corporation who would be delighted to assist them." Luce's relief whooshed out with his held breath. "Luce, do you normally get kinky video calls like this?"

"NO!" he half shouted. "I may have seduced hundreds of thousands of people, but every single one was hands-on, not through the use of technology like this." Oh Hell. Hardly the right thing to say at a time like this. Reminding Mel about his past indiscretions…

"Mel, now we're off the phone, what did she really say at the end? The generally unskilled bit?"

Mel frowned. "Are you sure you want me to repeat it? It wasn't very polite and some of it was quite crude." At Luce's nod, she said haltingly, "Your shrimp of a cock is tinier than my clit. No wonder you couldn't find it. If you'd fucked me all night, I wouldn't have even felt it, but you didn't have the stamina of my Dong and his massive cock. Yours must be worn to nothing from wanking every night because no woman will have you."

Luce was lost for words. Admittedly, just the sound of the words coming from Mel's perfect lips was a turn on, if they hadn't made him sound so…bad. He started the car to buy himself time before replying.

Mel spoke again before he could think of what to say. "What concerns me most is that Mr Han appeared to be about the same size as your thumb and his stamina lasted a grand total of two minutes and thirty-six seconds, including, ah, foreplay. His diminutive size and complete lack of stimulation to Mrs Han's erogenous zones in that very short time would suggest that her shrieks of pleasure were less than genuine. Her description of you is the complete opposite of my experience. In your time with Mrs Han, did you even take your pants off?"

"No," Luce admitted. "Didn't you watch the video? She swore she'd send it to Keiko. She was so drunk on wine and the prospect of letting her kinky side out that she didn't notice I used a —"

"NO! I don't need to know. As you say,

you've seduced many women and men, but I don't need the details of any of those encounters. The imps may enjoy observing, but I...don't." She handed him back his phone, shuddering, and he pocketed it.

A vivid flashback of the HELL Corporation Christmas party at the Hilton, the exotic dance routine from HR and Mel's acute embarrassment hit Luce like the logging truck barrelling along the highway. At the time, he'd been certain that all the wine she drank combined with the floor show would have aroused her. Instead, she'd downed an entire bottle of wine and stumbled out of the function room as if she was going to be sick. Now he felt sick at the memory.

"I'm sorry, Mel," he said quietly. "That you had to see that. That I had anything to do with that crazy woman. And...for everything. I'm sorry." He clicked on his indicator light and pulled out onto the highway, letting the car growl his anger at himself as they accelerated to match the speed limit on the otherwise deserted road.

Warm fingers covered his, pulling one hand

away from the steering wheel so Mel could clasp it between hers. "My love, sometimes the results of our actions are difficult to predict, especially when human free will comes into it. I arrived in Japan with the faint hope of persuading Mr Han to decide on a peaceful solution – one Koyane assured me he would never do. Your…actions with Mrs Han were never something I considered in my plans. Because of what you did, Mr Han chose the opposite course of action to spite her. I had my peaceful solution, but at the cost of Mr and Mrs Han's marriage and possibly their souls. Perhaps I was mistaken and the marriage was doomed anyway. I don't know. Something evidently drove her from his arms to yours." Her fingers trailed up to his shoulder. "Your very attractive arms, Luce, for your physical attributes border on the ideal to most women. And yet…the rift you helped create has brought the two of them back together again, to share what they both evidently enjoy. Sometimes Destiny smooths the way for things to play out as they should, however rough it may seem in the lead up." She squeezed his hand.

"You're not just talking about that crazy Korean couple any more, are you?"

"No, my love. My thoughts are much closer to home. The wonderful man beside me, taking me to our secluded loft apartment. Your magnificent body and your unparalleled skills in the bedroom. We've both been through Hell, but now we have the whole night ahead, with just the two of us and no need to worry about anyone else, let alone some other happy couple, half a world away." Her voice dropped to a whisper as he felt her hot breath. "I love you, Luce." She kissed his cheek and settled back in her seat.

Luce knew he had a dopey grin on his face, but he didn't care. Life didn't get much happier than this. Now, if he could just heal Mel a little more, maybe she'd be up for more when they reached the apartment. He reached for her hand and held it, sending a trickle of healing through their contact as he drove.

Half an hour later, he bumped onto the gravel drive to their accommodation. Dodging two kangaroos and a confused sheep, he pulled into the small parking lot and got out of the car. He trudged up the stairs without waiting for Mel, hoping to get the door unlocked so she wouldn't have to wait in the cold. Yet when he swung the door open, she wasn't beside him. He couldn't see her at all.

He jogged down the steps to the car and peered in. Mel still sat in the passenger seat, fast asleep.

Mel didn't know how much Destiny hated him. She'd never give Luce a smooth run if she could help it. Maybe he should have given in and spent a night with Destiny, back when he was still an angel, instead of ignoring the girl who was so far beneath him. Too late now.

He sighed and opened the door. Hoisting Mel in his arms, he kicked the car door shut and carried his precious, sleeping angel up the stairs to bed.

Fifteen

Mel woke to warmth, light and the aroma of something delicious. Once again, she felt more refreshed than any morning she'd awoken in Japan. It was either Australia or Luce responsible and she suspected she had Luce to thank. Not least of all for whatever was cooking.

She rose and padded quietly across the floor, admiring the well-muscled man so intent on the electric frying pan that he didn't notice she was up. She caught a glimpse of yellow and shifted her gaze from the drape of the silk of his boxer shorts over the little they covered, to his cooking. "Where did you get eggs? Ooh, and mushrooms."

Luce's lips lifted in a smile but he didn't do more than glance at Mel. The eggs required too much concentration, it seemed. "When I booked this place, I asked for a stocked kitchen. A selection of local produce for breakfast. I know you like a mushroom omelette, so I put the ingredients on the list. I spotted some bacon in the fridge, so when I get some fresh bread, I can do you a bacon sandwich."

Mel sighed happily, sinking onto the chaise. The first time in over a century that she'd seen one in a home. "Mmm, having my own personal, very sexy chef beats room service. Is there anything I can do to help?"

"No need. You just relax and let me take care of you." Luce deftly flipped, sizzled and sliced her breakfast in the pan, serving it on two plates that he set on the tiny table. He'd already laid the cutlery out with two glasses of juice. Waving around the table, he added,

"Breakfast is served. I can't find the coffee maker the website said was here, so it'll have to be juice until I can find a coffee shop in town. And ask the owner about the coffee maker." His eyes flashed darkly. "Everything here should be perfect for you and I don't want anyone spoiling it."

Mel slid into a wrought iron chair. "With or without coffee, this looks magnificent, my love. Thank you." She waited for him to sit down so she could lean forward to kiss him. "And my morning is perfect so far." She sliced a small bite of omelette and popped it into her mouth. "Mmm."

Luce shovelled a forkful of egg and mushroom into his own mouth and chewed moodily. He didn't say another word until he'd cleared his plate, shoved back from the table and clattered his dirty dishes into the sink. "I'm going into town to get coffee."

Mel watched in fascination as Luce grabbed his keys and opened the front door. A gust of wind fluttered his boxer shorts, making Mel reach for her jacket. Winters in Western Australia were cold, even without snow. Luce slammed the door shut and stomped across the floor to his suitcase. Several minutes later, the fully clothed Lord of Hell thundered down the stairs to the car park. A spray of dust and gravel marked his passage as he drove up to the road.

She finished her breakfast at a much more leisurely pace and decided to wash the dishes before leaving them to air-dry on the draining board. Next order of business was a shower and fresh clothes.

Mel had just finished braiding her damp hair when she heard a key in the door. Figuring Luce would be burdened with coffee, she crossed the room and opened the door for him.

"Oh, hello." Greg looked more surprised to see her than she was, but he also looked relieved. "I realised I forgot to bring up the new coffee machine yesterday. I found it sitting on the bench and thought I should give it to you right away." He held up the box, but didn't offer it to her.

"I'm not an expert with coffee machines," Mel admitted. "Luce is the one who knows what he's doing, but he's headed up to town to get coffee. You just missed him. It's probably best if you set it up and tell me how to use it."

After several minutes of flipping through the instruction book and peeling away packaging, Mel and Greg worked out that the coffee machine was surprisingly easy to use and she offered to make one for him.

He shook his head. "I should go. The cellar door downstairs opens for tasting in a few minutes and there's always someone who arrives right at ten on the dot." He hesitated, then ploughed on, "Look, I'm sorry I used the key instead of knocking, but I saw your…husband go out and I was working late last night, bringing some new stock up from the bottling room. I happened to glance outside when you and your husband returned and I saw him carrying what looked like your unconscious body upstairs. When he left without you this morning, I thought the worst and I had to check. I mean, your husband is a very…forceful man and he might have…done something." He reddened, as if embarrassed to be admitting any of this.

Mel took pity on him. "Luce isn't my husband. Neither of us is married. I'm Melody Angel – Mel." She offered her hand and he shook it. "Luce can be very intense sometimes and people do tend to get the wrong impression about him. He's very protective of me, especially at the moment, as I'm not well. He's brought me here for my health, in the hope that a holiday will help me recover. I fell asleep in the car last night and I woke up to find him being very gallant and carrying me up the stairs. So sweet of him. I didn't want to spoil it by making him put me down, so I let him continue without opening my eyes. He's surprisingly romantic when he wants to be, though I'd never tell him that. It'd completely ruin his tough-guy image."

Greg didn't look entirely convinced. "Look, if you need anything, or help with anything, or just need someone to talk to…come downstairs. Or up to the house, we're just on the other side of that paddock, hidden behind the trees. Tell him you want to try some nougat or something."

"Thank you, but I'm sure it won't be

necessary. You must get some very strange guests here if you're worried about Luce and me."

Greg shook his head. "You have no idea. Couples on their honeymoon seem to want to experiment. We had one couple buy the whole range of chocolate body products from the chocolate factory up the road. The sheets were streaked with it and there was chocolate all over the furniture, up the walls…even some handprints on the ceiling, from where we think they must have been jumping on the bed. The cleaning bill was astronomical. And then there was the couple who insisted on naked aerobics on the balcony every morning, finishing up with…well, they were on their honeymoon. Problem was, they didn't get up until ten and it's pretty hard to conduct wine tastings when you can hear the moans and groans on the balcony….not to mention the free show they gave everyone who drove up. You could see them from the car park."

Mel burst out laughing. "Oh my. We'll be well-behaved, I promise. No food in bed and none on the walls, either. I might take you up on the offer of nougat, though. I didn't get a chance to taste any yesterday. I might wait until Luce is in a better mood, though." She turned a beaming smile on the grumpy man framed in the open doorway. "Thank you, my love."

Luce ripped a cup out of the cardboard holder and held it out to Mel. "Your morning macchiato. I hope it's still hot – I had to drive for ages to find anywhere that was open. I got this from a coffee shop with cows everywhere, inside and out." He wrenched the lid off his own coffee and gulped half of the steaming liquid.

Only the Lord of Hell could do that without burning himself, Mel mused, sipping her own coffee carefully.

Greg grinned "So you got coffee in Cowaramup? That's why all the cows."

Luce glowered. "I wouldn't have had to if we had the coffee machine we were supposed to."

"We do now," Mel said smoothly. "Greg brought it up and was showing me how to use it. Apparently, the last guests broke the previous one so it's brand new. He was telling me about your romantic heroism last night – carrying your sleeping sweetheart up two flights of stairs to bed. Good thing you don't look dark and evil, or he'd have thought you were the villain instead, carrying me to your lair to ravish me." She struggled not to laugh when Luce looked down at his black shirt and her words started to sink in.

"I better get back to the cellar door. We're open for tastings," Greg said hurriedly, heading down the stairs at a trot.

Mel carefully closed the door behind him.

"He came up to check I hadn't murdered you, didn't he?" Luce crushed the empty coffee cup in his first and lobbed it at the rubbish bin.

Mel couldn't hold back her laughter any more. She nodded, unable to speak.

"I'm going down there now to tell him to keep his nose out of our business. He shouldn't be bothering you with his crazy ideas. I'll find somewhere else for us to stay and to Hell with this place."

"No. I like it here and he was only trying to help. Besides, I have a better idea." Mel couldn't resist a mischievous smile. "I think we should take a walk up to the chocolate factory we saw yesterday. He recommended some of their products that I'd dearly love to try with you."

Sixteen

At this rate, Mel's recovery would take years, Luce fumed, his fingers tightening around Mel's hand as they walked the familiar track home from the chocolate factory. Her soul had healed a little — from the scattered glitter he'd seen in his apartment, it was now a seamless golden glow haloing her body, but nowhere near the blinding radiance it should be. Even their short daily walk to the chocolate factory seemed to tax her and it'd been a whole week. He swung her bag of purchases in his free hand, not willing to let her carry even this light load. What was he doing wrong? Maybe he should have taken her to Heaven and let her heal there.

"It's all your fault," Mel chimed in, as if reading his mind. She smothered a small burp. "If you hadn't talked me into that brownie with ice cream, I wouldn't feel like a big, bloated ball you could roll all the way home. So much for sharing it with me. You barely had two bites – you fed the rest to me!"

Luce grinned. Of course he had. That blissful expression on her face after the first bite…could she blame him for wanting to see it again? Over and over again? "And you said I couldn't corrupt you."

Mel laughed. "I loved chocolate long before I loved you. You haven't corrupted me, my love. Seduced and tempted me, well, that's a very different matter. But you know I like the way you do it." There was both love and laughter in her kiss, which Luce wished lasted longer than it did.

Hell, they shared kisses and contact, but Luce could still feel her exhaustion and he knew he needed to be careful with her. He'd give anything for another night of passionate lovemaking with Mel, but he didn't dare take the risk yet. She still fell asleep in his arms every night, when he'd barely started to heal her. Maybe he wasn't healing her enough – he needed to do more, not stop when she fell asleep. Maybe…

Her fingers reached into his pocket, riveting him to the ground. Was she checking how tight his pants were? Just the thought of her…

Mel held up his phone, ringing with an incoming call from an unknown number. Luce hoped it wasn't the crazy Korean couple again. He'd unzip his pants and introduce them to the devil, he fumed. "Hello?" he growled, fumbling one-handed with his zip. "If you're calling to show me more R-rated videos, I'm not interested. I have my own, far more attractive lady here and she's –"

"Mel. She's Mel, I hope. If she isn't, you'd better tell me now," an Irish voice interrupted.

"Who's this?" Luce demanded, though he suspected he already knew.

"It's me, Patrick. I'm surprised you didn't

guess from my accent, Luce. Raphael has news, but he refused to call you himself, so he begged me to do it. He offered me all sorts of things, but I agreed because it'd give me an excuse to ask what I really want to know. How is she?" Even down the crackling mobile signal from the other side of the world, Luce could hear the concern in Patrick's voice.

Luce groped for Mel's hand and brought it to his lips. Her eyes turned to meet his and he struggled to read her soul through them. "She…she's not as strong as she should be, but she's a damn sight better than the sorry state she arrived home in. It's slow, but she's recovering. I've allowed a month, but I don't know if that will be enough."

Mel's eyes shimmered with tears at the pain and hopelessness even he could hear in his voice. "I trust you, my love. If anyone can help me recover, it's you. You'll find a way."

Patrick's voice came down the line again. "Is that her? Is she there? Can she hear me? Oh Hell, Mel, Koyane said he didn't think you'd last the flight home, but he thought persuading you to stay would only weaken you further. I wanted to fly over to help you, but there was a disturbance in Belfast that threatened to get ugly and I couldn't leave. Tell me how you did it."

She'd been so weak she almost didn't last the flight? No, the Mel who'd rescued him in the seminar room hadn't been on the verge of collapse. That was later, when Raphael had barged into his home. But if Koyane had been right, then why would she take such a risk to come here? Why wouldn't she stay in Japan until she was stronger?

"Luce."

Luce's eyes turned to Mel at the sound of his name on her lips.

"Luce. I came home for Luce."

She wasn't calling him – she was answering Patrick's question, which she must have heard. Luce hit the speakerphone button and held the phone up between them. "She's here," he said, "and she can hear you. I've put you on speakerphone. We're in a vineyard with no one nearby."

"Mel? How did you manage it?" Patrick asked.

"I had Luce waiting for me and he's with me now," Mel said simply. "He's been a Godsend, Patrick. I can't begin to enumerate half the things he's done for me this week and he picked the perfect location. All the locals think we're on our honeymoon. The minute they think Luce is out of earshot, the advice they whisper! You'd think half the people here are sex-mad and surprisingly kinky, too. One of them suggested I should…do all sorts of things to Luce." Her blush rivalled that chili rosé for its rosy colour.

"What sort of things?" Luce asked. Was there any chance they'd suggested something he'd fantasised about that Mel might be willing to do?

"I'm…not repeating them," Mel replied, still pink. "What news is there on Persi, Patrick?"

Damn.

Patrick stopped laughing. "Daniel reported that Persephone definitely was in Egypt – they found where she stayed, where she ate, all the tourist attractions she visited and where she shopped. And then…nothing. She disappeared without a trace about the time you were in

Japan, almost a fortnight ago. The trail's cold, so Daniel and the other Grigori came home. Raphael's sent word out to everyone he knows, though – any word of Persephone and he or Daniel will hear of it. Is there any chance…do you think she might be in Hell?"

"No. Every demon in Hell knows I don't want her there. If she takes so much as a single step inside Hell's gates, they know to bring her to me, or at least to the HELL Corporation. Mephi would have notified me if she had her." Luce glanced at Mel. "She's definitely not in Hell."

Mel's gaze rested on some distant trees. "If she's not in Hell…Patrick, has Raphael thought to look in Turkey or Greece? Or perhaps Italy?"

"You're reading my mind, Mel. Or has Raphael already told you? He's had three unconfirmed reports – one from Pamukkale in Turkey, one from some place in America and another from Sicily. He hasn't sent anyone in to investigate yet, though."

"Patrick, tell him to send someone to Pamukkale and to Enna in Sicily. When she was human, Persi lived in Sicily. She'd barely recognise the place now, but something tells me…that's where you need to be looking. She didn't like America much – she objected to something they called panties." Mel sighed, her shoulders slumping.

Luce hesitated as he took in Mel's tiredness before he said, "If there's nothing else for you to report, time to end the call. Mel's tired and I need to get her back home to rest."

Patrick coughed. "I'll call again if I hear more. Mel, please don't overdo it. You just concentrate on getting well. Luce…take care of her, okay? She's –"

"More precious than words can say," Luce finished for him. "Talk to you later, Patrick."

A round of goodbyes ended the call and Luce shoved his phone in his pocket again. Without asking her permission, he scooped Mel into his arms and strode back to the loft, ignoring the staring people in the car park.

Seventeen

Luce let Mel unlock the door before he kicked it open and carried her over the threshold. "The bed or the couch?" he demanded.

She laughed gently. "Neither, if you're going to be this grumpy. I don't make love with angry men." Luce opened his mouth to protest, but she waved him into silence. "I know you didn't mean it that way. I'd like to take an afternoon nap, so the bed's best, my love."

An afternoon nap? His fears were realised —

her health wasn't improving at all. She was deteriorating and there was nothing he could do to stop it. He had to abandon this stupid holiday idea and take her to Heaven where she'd be safe.

"Is it all right if we have dinner here instead of a restaurant? Pick up something from the freezer section of the shops in town and we can cook it in the kitchen here. I'll help when I wake up, I promise." Mel yawned so wide her hand barely covered her open mouth. "Sorry, Luce. I hope you didn't plan too much for this evening."

He forced a smile. "As long as I get to spend the evening with you, everything's going according to plan." The smile faded as fast as it had appeared. "Are you sure you'll be okay here without me?"

Mel had managed to strip off down to her knickers and a t-shirt and she was halfway through burrowing under the quilt. "I'll be fine. Fast asleep, probably. Wake me when you return. The way you know I like it."

A kiss, the rousing sort normally reserved for princesses in fairy tales. "I wouldn't have it any other way." Luce leaned down to kiss her gently – more goodbye than good morning, but at least he got one. "You just rest, all right?" Mel nodded and settled deeper into the pillow. Luce stretched an arm out to snag the curtain, pulling it shut across the section of window closest to the bed. It wasn't a night-time gloom, but it might help her sleep.

He took the stairs two at a time, surprising a group of wine tasters who were just leaving the cellar door. He recognised some of them as the people who'd gaped as he carried Mel up the stairs twenty minutes earlier. Luce managed a grin and a wink as he said, "Just heading into town for some supplies."

One of the women sniggered and whispered something to the man next to her.

Luce climbed into his car and sped away before he wasted any more time. The little town nearby didn't have much in the way of groceries, so for a decent dinner it was an hour round trip, plus however long he'd be in the shop. Mel would definitely have time for her afternoon nap before he returned.

Ninety-three minutes later, he decelerated

for the little gravel driveway that would return him to Mel. He made his way silently up the steps and into the darkened loft without waking her, so he tried to fill the fridge and freezer with his purchases as quietly as possible. Surveying the packed freezer, he figured he had more little dim sum morsels that could be baked, fried and steamed than Mel could eat in a week, with enough sauces for the things to swim in, but he figured it'd be better to give her a choice than risk giving her something she wouldn't eat. There wasn't an oyster in sight.

He poured two glasses of wine and tasted a mouthful of his. Pretty decent, considering. With the berries, tannins and whatever else still lingering on his tongue, Luce stepped into the bedroom. He knelt beside the bed and took Mel in his arms. Luce started with a light kiss, then drove deeper as Mel's lips parted to emit a contented sigh. His tongue stroked hers, coaxing her to wake, until he felt her respond fully. Her fingers crept into his hair as one hand circled the back of his neck.

"Mmmm," she sighed, pressing her cotton-clad breasts against his chest.

He held her so tight he thought he might crush her, kissing her as if she could be taken away from him at any moment. She could — she could! But right now, she was in his arms. "Melody. Oh, Melody. I want…I want…"

She laid a warm finger against his lips. "I know, my love. So do I. How about after dinner?"

Luce grinned. "You'll be the sweetest dessert ever." He helped her out of bed and watched wistfully as she wrapped herself in a bathrobe. He made a mental note to switch the heating on when he got a moment, so she'd shed the bathrobe when the apartment was warm enough. The cold crept in quickly of an evening out here.

Together, they decided to cook a selection from each of the frozen food boxes, so they'd know what was best. Luce loaded an oven tray while Mel boiled water for the steamer. Mel set the sauces out in saucers on the table and Luce caught sight of her dipping her finger in a wine-coloured one to taste it. God, he wanted to be the one licking her finger. Later, he reminded himself.

It started out simple – when the food was ready, they dished it up onto a couple of plates in the middle of the table. Then they dipped the bite-sized pieces into the sauce dishes before devouring them. It lasted until Mel let out a moan. "Oh, you have to try one of these." She snagged a dumpling, dipped it in the dark red sauce and lifted it to Luce's lips. "Oops."

Luce managed to get the whole saucy morsel into his mouth, but he followed her gaze to the blotch of burgundy on his grey shirt. Bugger. Oh well, it was just a shirt. He swallowed and said, "My turn." He picked up a tiny spring roll and dunked it into the nearest sauce dish. The roll touched her lips before he lost control of the chopsticks and it narrowly missed Mel's left breast as it landed on the tablecloth and rolled, leaving a streak of brown behind. "Oh Hell, I'm so sorry." Luce swiped at it with the tea towel, but he only succeeded in spreading the mess further.

Mel laughed. "I guess we'll have to do some laundry soon. Not tomorrow, though. Nothing will dry in the rain."

Luce stopped with his sweet-chili-coated money-bag halfway to his mouth. "It's going to rain tomorrow? How do you know?"

"Weather forecasting? Luce, even humans can predict the future when it comes to weather. For me, that's easy." Mel popped the last dumpling into her mouth and smiled.

Could she really read the future? Luce wondered. He vaguely recalled her mentioning it before, but he'd dismissed it at the time. "You can predict what's going to happen?" he asked. At her nod, he ploughed on. "Do you know what our future holds? How you manage to recover and whether it's me that helps you do it? Whether…whether we ever get to be happy together, or will everyone keep interfering until you give me up as a waste of your precious time?" He hadn't meant to say quite that much, but the words had escaped now, to haunt him forever.

Mel patted her mouth with a serviette and dropped it on her plate, then rose and held out her hand. Luce took it without thinking. "Come here, Luce." She crossed to the couch and sat, pulling Luce to the cushion beside her. As Mel tilted her head up, her grey eyes captured his. "I can read the future for anyone but myself — and that means yours, too, for your future is so closely woven with mine that it's nearly impossible to separate them. I know I'll manage to recover because I know you — and you won't let me fade away to nothing. Whether it's here or Heaven or somewhere else entirely, I know you'll take better care of me than anyone else could. As for happiness — I know I'm happy here with you, right now. If you're not, you should tell me because I love you and your happiness means a lot to me, Luce."

Caught, he couldn't deny her anything — least of all the truth. "I love you. I'm the happiest I've ever been because I'm with you, Mel."

They shared a kiss, but Luce pulled her against him before she could move away. "Please. Just let me hold you for a bit longer." He felt Mel relax into his embrace and this time he didn't hesitate. He started healing her as soon as he could summon the energy. Mel didn't protest, so he intensified the flow. It was getting easier every day, but it wasn't enough, he knew.

Dinner was cold and congealed on his plate by the time he tore his focus from Mel. She was limp, lying across his lap, fast asleep. That made it the seventh night in a row he'd started healing her and she'd drifted off, every time. He forced down his disappointment – her health was far more important than how much he wanted sex. Gently, he untied her bathrobe and lifted her out of it, carrying her back to bed.

Most nights, he just tucked her in and watched TV until he was tired enough to join her. Not tonight. This time, he was going to try and keep healing her in the hope that he could make a difference. If he couldn't help her regain her strength, he'd have to take her to Heaven and their holiday would be over.

He prayed for help, for guidance and for the guts to do whatever she needed him to do. Even if that meant going away and leaving her forever.

Eighteen

Luce squinted in the light that seemed to beam into his eyes and rolled over so the sun would leave him alone. The curtain confused him, though – where was the bright sunlight coming from, if it wasn't the window? He sat up and realised it was Mel that had blinded him – standing in the kitchen, wearing nothing but her white t-shirt and underwear, caught in a ray of sunlight from the section of window where the curtains were wide open. Even as he watched, the light dimmed so he could see her clearly again.

"Good morning, my love," she said, turning to poke something in the electric frypan. Something that sizzled.

Luce sniffed and recognised bacon. He was in Heaven. Heaven with a near-naked Melody and a future that included bacon sandwiches. Holy Hell, she was an absolute angel. The sweetest angel who'd ever lived. He needed to thank her. And kiss her.

He'd crossed the floor and his arms were closing around her before he'd finished the thought. Luce deposited a line of kisses on the back of her neck until she tilted her head back to look up at him.

"Good morning," she repeated.

"Mm," he responded, not wanting to untangle his tongue from hers to give a more coherent response. He hadn't imagined it. Sunlight hadn't been the only thing making Mel glow – her soul was brighter this morning. He'd finally done something right. Something that had helped her recover.

She laughingly broke the kiss. "I'll burn the bacon!"

"Can't have that," he drawled, reaching into the cupboard for some plates. He set the table while she cooked, so that when Mel brought the plate of bacon, everything else was ready, too, including her coffee.

The bacon was cooked to perfection – like everything Mel did, Luce mused, his mouth full of his Heavenly breakfast.

"So, what's the plan for today?" Mel asked. "With the weather what it is, I'd say our walk to the chocolate factory is cancelled."

He hadn't heard the pattering on the roof over the sizzling bacon, but now he could see the rain streaming down the windows and the skylight. Hell, what had he planned for their trip? "Um…for a rainy day, I'd planned a visit to the caves and some wine tasting." He watched her carefully, hoping he'd picked right.

Mel's slight frown made his stomach churn. "Wine tasting? I'm not sure I could do that right after breakfast. In the afternoon, maybe…"

Luce breathed again. "So we explore the caves this morning and do wineries in the afternoon?"

Mel beamed. "That sounds like a wonderful plan. Tasting to find the perfect bottle of wine to share in the spa tonight." She winked. "When were you planning on letting me use the spa? We've been here a week and I've been dying to spend some time immersed in hot water and bubbles. It looks like there's room for you, too."

Was she well enough to start doing touristy things? Luce wondered. Or would a day of sightseeing only exhaust her further? "Are you sure you're up for this?"

Mel squeezed his hand. "You're not doing it without me, my love. I'm certainly up for this."

Nineteen

Luce waved Mel over, unable to stop staring and unsure what to make of it. "Hey, Mel. It looks like a rhinoceros slept with a wombat. A Zygo…*Zygomaturus trilobus.*"

Her head emerged from the collar of her white sweater – she'd insisted on going back to the car to get it, though the guy at the ticket desk had said that the cave wasn't cold – and she burst out laughing. "If I remember correctly, that creature predates them both." She took Luce's arm and lowered her voice.

"The ones here didn't look like that, either. They had short, bristly hair and it was more rust-coloured than that. Only the mountain ones were grey."

Luce debated whether to tell the ranger, back at the ticket counter. No, Mel wouldn't let him mess with the man.

"And one of the best spit roasts I've ever tasted," she continued quietly.

"Just how long have you been coming here on your holidays?" Luce asked, trying to match her voice's volume.

Mel shrugged. "Since people first came here, or maybe before."

"How long?"

"I don't know for sure. How long have those things been extinct?"

Luce leaned over to read the sign. "Fifty thousand years."

"A while, then."

He pulled her to the edge of the boardwalk, away from the statue of the extinct creature that Mel had eaten as a spit roast. "You can't just throw statements out like that and expect me to ignore them. Mel, I've only been here five. Five, since…since I fell." He swallowed and continued, "How did you manage to stay here that long and not be corrupted? I mean, after what happened to the first Grigori…they went native after only a few years! And yet you…you…"

Her eyes held sadness. "I watched, I lived and I learned. I experienced but never let it consume me. Humans are my responsibility and I sought to understand them better so that I could provide appropriate advice. One of them, yet always apart because I knew I wasn't one of them. Always."

"Like me in Hell," Luce breathed. "Surrounded yet alone. Never being a part of their society because what you are sets you apart. And they can never know." He hugged her tightly, finally understanding the loneliness that had driven his precious angel into his arms. He wasn't perfect or even good – but he was a kindred spirit of sorts.

Mel's unsquashable smile returned as she pulled away from him. "Yes, we have our similarities, my love. But I wouldn't call sleeping with thousands of them alone, by any stretch of the imagination." She winked and approached the cave entrance, where the aging stalactites looked like grey teeth about to devour her.

Luce hurried to catch up. "It's not like they were all at the same time. Sometimes two, rarely three and on one, glorious occasion, four. I bet you never got that close to any of them."

"What will you bet, Luce?"

He faltered. "I don't believe it." Mel wouldn't gamble when she knew she'd win, surely. "Not you. Not the untainted angel."

Her blush was just visible as they entered the cave. "I advise those in power or those who will be on how best to use that power. And for one man, that included…his…skill for enchanting women." She strode into the dark.

No. She wasn't getting away with dropping this bombshell and walking away. "Mel, please tell me his name." Don't let it be Patrick. He liked the saint well enough, but he wasn't sure he could tolerate him if he knew the man had been Mel's lover for centuries, let alone her one and only, legendary human lover.

"Gaius. His praenomen was Gaius."

Not Patrick, though still a Latin name. "Is he an angel?"

"No."

Luce breathed again. "So tell me his nomen and the rest. A legendary lover and leader wouldn't have less than three names in the Roman Empire."

"Republic. He was a man of the Roman Republic. There was no empire in his lifetime."

"Mel…"

She sighed. "All right. Gaius Julius Caesar. He was young and he didn't believe he'd ever achieve his ambitions, though he hid his feelings well. He was also a very eager student. A rare human, but he didn't understand how short-sighted other humans can be. Politicians still make decisions in the heat of the moment, without considering consequences. He believed me to be a goddess, of sorts."

Luce snorted. "Venus, I'm sure. Isn't that incest? He was descended from Venus, or he said he was."

Mel shrugged. "He wasn't my descendant, so what does it matter? I've never had a child.

Never needed to. I have enough to care for."

"Never wanted to, either?" Luce pressed. Curiosity had dug its claws into him and with Mel in a communicative mood, he was happy to give his desire for answers a long leash.

"No. I inhabit a body that's perfect in every way, except that. I cannot commit to the nine months it will take to bear a child to term, then the twenty years after to properly raise it to adulthood. And it would be human – mortal, until its first life is complete. Only after death would it be able to understand what it truly was. I'm lucky if I know where I will be required from week to week, let alone two decades. If circumstances required me to give my life for someone, I would do so – my body is replaceable. But a baby is not. It is a small sacrifice, perhaps, but not one I think on often. I have cared for children of all ages – I don't need one born from my loins." She sighed.

"I bet they're all paragons of angelic virtue, too."

The pain in her eyes told him he'd guessed wrong for the second time. "I raised Michael and I was responsible for Persephone after Hades…after…I…I'm sorry, Luce. Can we not discuss this? I want to enjoy this cave in your company and not think about all that awaits me when our holiday is over. Can we talk about the cave instead, please?"

"Sure." No wonder she didn't want to talk about children – she'd dealt with the most difficult people he could think of. He could feel her weariness as she took his arm. Please, not yet! he prayed. Their day together had barely begun. It was much too early to end it. "Did you know the water in caves has filtered through soil and rock for thousands of years before it becomes the pure pools inside the cave? Come swim in it with me." He nodded at the pool inside the entrance of Mammoth Cave and made short work of his shirt buttons. Mel's eyes lingered on his chest as he slid his shirt off.

She blinked and shook her head. "I'm not swimming in that. It's shallow, seasonal and full of mud. Not one of your pure, filtered pools." She grabbed the tiny torch she'd been given at the ticket office and flicked it on. The light beam played across a distinctly brown pool that was only a few inches deep.

"Maybe deeper inside, then," Luce insisted, pulling his shirt back on. "The photos of this place showed plenty of water."

Each pool Mel shone her light on was as disappointing as the first. Luce had seen his fill of stalactites, stalagmites and…he still wasn't convinced that the weird conglomeration of flowstone looked like a mammoth, but he hadn't taken Mel for a swim and it was chafing at him. When they reached the exit sign, Luce stomped down the steps. At the base, he finally found the source of the water – not a spring or centuries of ceiling drips, but a stream running down the collapsed doline and into the cave. No wonder it was shallow and muddy – it was recent rainwater runoff.

He sighed, trudging along the stream until daylight blazed overhead, illuminating the maze of stairs that led to the world above. For a moment, he felt like he was in the lowest levels of Hell, looking up at the distant circle of sky, rimmed by tree-topped cliffs. The warmth of Mel at his side made him itch to break out his wings and fly her to the surface in his arms. He could bear to take her to Heaven like this. Secure in his embrace, maybe he'd be able to let her go.

Damp lips touched his cheek. "No," Mel whispered. Luce was surprised to see tears streaming down her face. "We're taking the stairway. Together."

Luce chuckled. He hadn't realised Mel was a Zeppelin fan. "Only if you're sure." He gave an extravagant bow. "Ladies first." He watched Mel's slow ascent, staying a step below her in case she faltered, but she didn't stop until they reached the heavy metal gate at the top, marking the end of the steel and timber staircase and the start of the stone steps cut into the cliff.

The path ended abruptly in gravel and bitumen – the highway, Luce realised. They hurried across before a car could come around the corner. The track on the other side forked into a scenic walk and the direct path to the exit, the sign said, but the difference in distance was only a few hundred metres. "The scenic route?" Luce asked and Mel nodded. He curled his arm around her waist and they took the left fork.

Twenty

Rounding the first corner, they were greeted by a length of rope tied between two bushes. A hastily handwritten sign swimming in a sodden plastic folder said:

Track closed due to rain.

The clearing skies belied the words – it wouldn't rain again until they were well past this place.

Luce looked at Mel. "Well, that sure looks official," he said, lifting the rope to let her pass underneath. He followed, brushing aside a spider's web that stretched across the track. Evidently the other visitors had fallen for the sign and taken the boring route back to the car park.

Birds chattered loudly overhead, invisible in the canopy far above. Were they laughing at him or warning him? He looked askance at Mel.

"Ring-neck parrots," she said, raising her eyes. "Noisy!" she addressed them and they responded with another melodic chorus that made her laugh. She stepped into a patch of sunlight and time stood still. Her mussed hair and fluffy white sweater caught the light, haloing her like the angel she truly was.

Too good for him, Luce told himself, forcing his feet to move forward. The track turned oddly green and blue and Luce didn't have time to process what that meant before he was ankle-deep in the pool that had reflected the sky until he splashed into it. He squelched out just in time to stop Mel from making the same mistake.

"Look, there's stepping stones," Mel said,

pointing.

Not stones so much as sawn-off sections of tree trunks, but they probably served the same purpose, Luce decided. He hesitated for an instant before sweeping Mel off her feet and into his arms. Over her laughter, he said, "I want to be a gentleman and carry you across. Now, are you going to let me or not?"

Mel inclined her head. "That's very sweet of you. Of course I will, Luce."

Three steps in, he regretted his gallant gesture. The wet wood was slippery, and carrying Mel messed with his balance. The water slopping out of his soaked shoes didn't help, either. He had to stretch for the fourth one and it wobbled under his foot, then tipped over and threw him into the pool. He landed painfully on his hip, sending water splashing onto the bushes. The water was just deep enough to soak him completely, but Mel had somehow landed partially on top of him and partly on a wide stepping stone that sat just above the surface.

She rose and planted her feet firmly on the slippery wood. Mel spread her arms wide, her sympathetic eyes looking down on him from where she stood, high and secure on her pedestal. Her clothes were immaculate and her shoes looked like they'd received one tiny droplet between them. Even as he watched, it rolled down the surface of her sneaker. Just like the day they met – he and Lili were covered in coffee and none of it touched her.

An angel who could live among humans for fifty thousand years and not be tainted. Next to her, he was nothing.

"Take my hand, Luce, and I'll help you rise."

God, how much he wanted to, but maybe it was time to face facts. "How many times do I have to stumble and fall, Mel, before you won't help me any more?"

She laughed, leaned down and grasped his hands, lifting him effortlessly to his feet. "As many times as it takes for you not to stumble ever again."

Luce snorted, looking down at the water that lapped his knees. "I'll never be perfect, Mel."

Her fingers wove between his and she leaped for the next timber island. She tugged at his arm until Luce splashed to her side. "You don't need to be." Her feet glided to the next step…and the next, as Luce sloshed along beside her. "And I will always come to help you. Another fifty thousand years and more. Until the world ends or you no longer need me."

They reached the bank without further incident and Luce had had enough. The way his wet pants clung to him as he walked felt way too tight. They had to go. And if the pants went, damned if he was wearing any of the rest of it. He made quick work of his clothes and shoes, bundling them up and shoving them under his arm.

With one baleful glance at the once again reflective pool, Luce set off down the track, stark naked.

Mel's footsteps sounded softly behind him. "Aren't you cold, Luce?"

"No," he snapped. "As long as I'm the Lord of Hell and I'm this pissed off, snow will turn to steam on my skin." As if to illustrate his point, a wisp of steam rose from the wet clothes under his arm.

"So you don't mind if I walk behind you instead of beside you, so I can admire your arse? Seeing as it's on display and all."

Luce grinned and swung his hips as he walked, unable to resist giving Mel a good show. Right up until he tripped on a big rock sticking out of the soil and landed on a particularly prickly bush. Some sort of stunted palm tree. What kind of palm tree lived in a freezing cold West Australian forest, lurking in wait to slice up passers-by? Luce swore until he ran out of breath.

Above, the parrots cackled again and it sounded suspiciously like laughter. Luce swore at them, too.

Mel's hands snaked around his torso, yanking him out of the knife-edged leaves and against her soft, clothed body instead. A few deft touches sealed his cuts and the only remaining injury was to his pride. Which he didn't have anyway, he fumed, because the imp thought it was an illusion.

"Would you like me to summon clothes for you, my love? I'm cold just looking at you. Even though…well…" She blushed as her eyes drifted down.

It's not like he had any pride left to lose. "Yes," he bit out, then added a softening, "Please. If it's not too much for you, Mel. If it is, I'll be fine until we get to the car. I always keep spare clothes there."

She screwed her face up in concentration and Luce felt the slight change in air current across his skin. The pants were thick, grey cotton, but the t-shirt was much softer and lighter. He felt Mel slump against him.

No. He pivoted and caught her before she fell.

"I'm sorry," Mel whispered, waving at his yellow shirt. "It's all I could manage."

"It's more than enough," he replied, realising that the pants and shirt really were all she'd summoned — his feet were bare and he was comfortably commando. He lifted her in his arms again. "This time, I won't fall."

He strode confidently along the remainder of the track, pausing to glare at the official sign that declared the track closed. Where was the official sign at the other end, where it was needed? Muttering, he swept past it to take

Mel to the car.

He patted down his pockets in search of his keys, before realising that everything – his car keys, wallet and phone – was still with his wet clothes, which he'd dropped during his fight with the guerrilla palm tree.

"Go back and get them. I'll be fine here," Mel said, sinking onto the timber barrier that marked the border between car park and bush.

Luce nodded and set off at a run. The feel of damp leaves and soil under his feet was oddly refreshing. He kept his eyes on the ground so he wouldn't be ambushed by another camouflaged rock. He couldn't remember how long it had been since he ran barefoot anywhere. Hooves in Hell and expensive shoes everywhere else. The more time he spent with Mel, the more he found himself doing things differently…and he couldn't deny he liked it.

He found his clothes lying in a heap behind a shrub smothered in a purple flowering vine. His shoes, phone and wallet were there, too – everything except his keys. Swearing, Luce looked around, but there was no glint of metal to be seen. He kicked at the leaf litter, stirring up what seemed like a million surprisingly large creepy-crawlies, but no keys.

He glared at the deceptively pretty pool. Surely he hadn't dropped his keys in there. Oh Hell, if he had…

Good thing Mel hadn't given him shoes. The drill pants were easy to roll up past his knees so Luce could wade into the cold water, combing through the mud with his toes. Twice he seized things that scuttled away in the water and he wondered idly what they'd taste like, steamed and sauced for dinner. Next time he saw marron on the menu, he'd order it. Especially if the bloody things had buried his keys.

After twenty minutes of digging his toes through every inch of the pool with nothing to show for it, he stomped back to the car. At least he had his phone – he could call Mephi to arrange for a spare set of keys and someone to search the whole damn national park for them. With metal detectors.

He had to wait for a tourist coach to pass, gears grinding over the low rumble of its engine, before he could cross the road to where Mel was sitting beside a pair of birds. One launched into the chattering, musical melody he'd heard when he fell into the pool. So those were ring-neck parrots, he thought, deciding that their black heads perfectly matched their mocking black hearts for laughing at his misfortune.

As he approached Mel, the green birds took flight, skimming just over his head as they hooted. He wanted to swat the noisy nuisances out of the air, but Mel's sweet smile somehow softened his anger a little. Enough not to kill a couple of birds, anyway.

"Did you find everything?" she asked, nodding at the bundle in his hands.

"Everything but my damn keys," he answered. "I'll call the office and get someone to bring the spares down. At least I found my wallet, so I can get you a drink from the ticket office while you're waiting."

Mel lifted her arm. The silvery glitter as the keys caught the sunlight made him wonder how Mel had managed to summon them to her when he hadn't been able to find them at all. "They were still in my pocket from when I went to get my sweater."

Luce snatched them with a relieved, "Thank you," and deactivated the central locking.

While Mel slid into the passenger seat, he popped the boot to find some suitable footwear. He'd always kept a couple complete sets of clothes – one casual, one business – in there, just in case he spent a night away and needed them in the morning. He had an image to uphold and barefoot didn't cut it. He fingered the set of casual clothes that had been bagged up with his less shiny pair of shoes. Black, of course, and a lot smarter-looking than Mel's gift of hiking clothes. Funny how she turned things her signature colour when she was tired. He'd treasure the gold sheets and towels in his lair in Hell, if he ever returned to pack his things before the new bloke took over, whoever that was.

Luce lifted the hem of his t-shirt and sniffed the butter-coloured fabric. She'd been nestled against his chest, so it was no surprise that the scent of her perfume lingered. In one smooth movement, he pulled the shirt over his head, folding it neatly before placing it in the front pocket of the bag of clean clothes. He wouldn't be wearing this precious shirt today — he wanted to keep it safe.

The black, HELL Corporation polo shirt was rough against his skin — hardly the soft cotton Mel had chosen for him. He thought about changing his pants and possibly putting some underwear on, and he undid the button on his pants, sliding them over his hips.

"Keep going, big boy!" an elderly voice cackled.

Luce glanced in the direction the catcall had come from. The pensioners milling around the coach were watching him avidly.

"Oh my, do you think he's going to bare himself right here? I'll call my son. He's a police officer. He'll have him charged for indecency…"

Oh Hell. While ordinarily he wouldn't mind baring his arse and all his bits to any admirer, even the appreciative elderly crowd, Luce knew getting arrested would spoil Mel's day. He pulled the pants back up and fastened them again to howls of disappointment from the onlookers. He grinned and waved as he slammed the lid shut and carried his shoes to the driver's seat so he could put them on.

As soon as he closed the door, Mel said, "I'm sorry about the shirt. I know it's not your colour. I'll change it when I'm feeling a little…stronger."

Luce reached for her hand, squeezing her fingers as he tried to heal her without her noticing. He figured he was getting better at this because she didn't tell him to stop. "Don't you dare. It's your colour and it's perfect as it is. I don't want to get it dirty, is all, in case I fall into any more creeks today. It's safely wrapped up in the boot." Despite sitting in the sun while they were underground and tramping through the bush, the car's interior was decidedly chilly. Luce reached over and clicked the heater on.

"If you say so," Mel responded. "Where to next?"

Luce grinned and backed out of the parking bay, not saying a word.

Twenty-one

A few minutes after they reached Caves Road, Luce turned off it again. Mel seemed happy to maintain the silence, so he kept his mouth firmly closed until they pulled up outside a modern building. When they got out of the car, she eyed him askance over the dark roof.

"I could do with a coffee," he admitted, jerking his head toward the tearooms next door. Mel nodded and that's where they headed.

Luce ordered his standard espresso and

looked expectantly at Mel.

"Ooh, they have milkshakes with ice cream," she exclaimed, her eyes on the menu.

The man behind the counter grinned. "We sure do. They're a legend in these parts."

Luce laughed. "You want a milkshake instead of a coffee? Are you sure you won't fall asleep on me?"

Mel lifted her chin. "I'll have both. A milkshake and a macchiato, please."

"What flavour?" When the man saw Mel's blank look, he started reeling off a list of choices.

Mel managed a smile. "Vanilla, please. And only half as much syrup – I'm not all that sweet. Hell, the milk and the ice cream alone are enough for me."

Luce let his raised eyebrows convey his disbelief. Had he caught her in a lie? He paid for their drinks, keeping his eyes on Mel's deepening blush. It wasn't a lie if she didn't believe she was sweet. He returned his credit card to his wallet and pulled Mel over to a table by the window.

He leaned across the table and kissed her,

not letting up until the sounds of coffee and milkshake making were loud enough to hide his words. "Sweetest angel I ever tasted." When he pulled back, he grasped her hands instead, reaching automatically for her soul. Damn. This morning's brightness had faded as if a whole night's rest had never happened. At least he could heal her body and reduce the stress on her soul that way.

Luce glanced up to find Mel's eyes on him. Unfathomable grey depths he longed to lose himself in. Her voice was a seductive whisper. "Sweetest devil I ever tasted, and the sweetest angel, too." She lifted their joined hands and kissed his. "Taking such good care of me."

He searched her eyes for a double meaning – should he take the words at face value or was it her idea of a gentle rebuke for the setbacks from his stumbling this morning? Doubt settled like a stone in his stomach. "I'm sorry," he mumbled.

Their drinks arrived and Mel made short work of the frothy, white, milk concoction. Luce was barely halfway through his coffee when she nudged the empty cup aside and slid her macchiato closer.

She smiled at his stunned expression and leaned closer to whisper, "Kiss me and see if I'm any sweeter."

How could he refuse? Luce tasted the piercing note of vanilla on her lips and the ice cream chill lingered on her tongue. The forced sweetness from the sugar was nothing compared to his Melody – no, not even if she'd drunk the whole bottle of syrup. He licked his lips and grinned. "No. You couldn't be."

She snorted softly into her coffee.

When they were done, they rose together and proceeded through the squeaky glass door to the near-noon sunshine outside.

The bigger building next door proclaimed its purpose as the ticket office for Lake Cave and the cave museum for the region. The breeze had picked up, slamming the door behind Luce before he could pull it shut. At the counter, Luce asked for two tickets, expecting another mp3-player guided tour like the one they'd been offered at Mammoth Cave which allowed them to explore the cave at their leisure.

"You've just missed the last tour. Next one's in two hours, at one," the cheerful man in ranger's greens told them.

Luce waved away the thought of a tour. He and Mel didn't need some human pointing out the difference between a stalagmite and a stalactite as they described rocks as various parts of his anatomy. The suggestive stalagmites in Mammoth Cave had been funny at first, but some of them were disturbingly accurate in both size and shape. As if some mocking imp had sneaked in and sculpted the damn things. "Just two tickets. No tour guide needed."

The ranger coughed out a laugh. "I'm sorry, sir, but you don't get in to Lake Cave without a tour. And the next one's at 1pm."

Luce squinted at the obstructive government employee. He sounded like one of the HELL Corporation demons. If he was, then he'd recognise him and soon change his tune. He leaned over the counter with his best authoritative stare. "Don't you know who I am?"

"Nope!" the man replied cheerfully. "And it won't matter if you're mining magnate Ginger Rhinestone, the Prime Minister or the Queen herself. Not even Satan would dare interrupt Sandy, today's tour guide, while she's on her lunchbreak, or she'll slip up and tell all the tour groups the real name of Satan's Little Finger."

Those damn imps got everywhere, Luce fumed. But he still wanted to take Mel into the cave. This one had to be better than the last one — after all, it had a lake. It said so on the sign. "Two tickets for one o'clock, please," he said grudgingly. And if the tour guide dared call a cave formation anything but his finger, well…he'd show her the cave's scale representations were woefully inadequate when compared to the reality.

They wandered through the museum, looking at photos of caves Luce recognised as adjacent to some of the caverns of Hell. He'd gone exploring on occasion, during the many boring millennia, and even caused a collapse once while there were humans inside. He heard that some big Hollywood director had made a movie about that — but he'd bet no one on the film crew knew about his involvement in the incident. He hoped Mel didn't, either.

Luce glanced at his watch. They still had over ninety minutes to kill.

"How about we follow the tour guide's example and have an early lunch?" Mel suggested. "I really liked some of the things on the tearooms' menu. The barramundi burger looked tempting."

Time to return to the tearooms.

Twenty-two

The barramundi burger had been bloody good, if a bit too big for Mel. He'd had to finish the last of hers for her. Now they only had thirty minutes to kill and, leaning over the railing to survey an even deeper collapsed doline, some of that would be spent on the descent. More stairs.

Mel's hand touched his arm. "My love, tell me how many people are here for the tour."

He shrugged. "I didn't ask. Does it matter?"

She laughed softly. "Seek out their souls,

Luce, and tell me what you find."

It was an odd request, but not a difficult one. Human souls had a balance of darkness and light, a little like his used to before Mel had helped him burn away the darkness. The difference was that the darkness was generally a part of their own soul and not some other soul trying to take over. He started counting the energy signatures. "Six…seven…no, nine."

"Eight," Mel whispered. "One is the ranger in the ticket office. What can you tell me about them?"

"None of them are completely damned," he replied quickly. A flicker of red across one soul made him reconsider. This was an odd soul. The darkness in this one was more red than black, marking the soul as a violent killer, but the darkness was wispy and faint compared to the brightness of this soul. Like wine dripped into water. A reformed killer? One who'd spent their time in prison, regretting their crimes, but who still felt the urge for violence? "And…one of them is a convicted killer who could kill again."

"Sometimes death is justified," Mel replied,

as if hinting at depths he hadn't seen.

"Like in war?" Luce guessed.

Mel looked grave. "Look again, Luce. At the soul and the body wearing it."

Luce focussed on the strange soul's signature and turned to look at the soldier. His jaw dropped open as he realised he was staring at a petite teenage girl. From her olive skin and dark, alluring eyes, he figured she was from somewhere in the Middle East. "A child soldier? A terrorist?"

Mel was silent, so Luce crossed the boardwalk to get a better look at the teenager. Her clothes were tailored to her body, so it didn't look like she was carrying weapons or explosives. If she was a terrorist, she wasn't on duty today.

The door to the museum opened and a man stepped out. Luce placed him at close to thirty, with the physique of someone who put in hours at the gym. Yet his soul matched the girl's — red and black intertwined, but where hers held more light, his leaned toward darkness. Yet that wispy red thread wove through it, disappearing into the darkness only to reappear somewhere else without warning.

This one was a soldier, surely. One whose guilt over every death dragged him down into a mire of despair. Not damned, but headed there. Especially if he turned those killer instincts on himself.

The girl's eyes were on him. Was he her target?

The wind slammed the visitor centre door and the soldier ducked for cover as if training was instinct. Luce had seen similar behaviour in veterans during fireworks displays in America.

"Well he looks like he's one wrong word away from suicide," Luce remarked to the girl. "I haven't seen a case of PTSD that bad since the Fourth of July in the US. Where do you bet he was stationed, Afghanistan or Iraq?"

She looked shocked, her eyes darting from the soldier to Luce. Those dark, doe eyes flashed like a night-time thunderstorm as she bit out, "There are worse things than war that can do that to a man."

Luce waited for her to elaborate, but she didn't. Snarky teenager. What was she to him?

The soldier had to be twice her age, but he didn't look old enough to be her father. "So you're his friend – girlfriend, maybe?" Satisfaction at being right made him grin at her defensive reaction. "Get out while you can. You don't want to be the one to find him when he offs himself. No one needs to –"

Mel's lips cut him off with a delicious kiss. "My love, are you scaring people? Maybe we should have spent the day at home."

She was probably right – she'd have been better off resting in bed and he wouldn't have ended up in the creek. The girl was still staring at him, though, so Luce figured he'd mess with her a little more and maybe even make Mel blush. "Hey, if you want to chain me to the bed, you know I'm up for that, Mel. Like I said –" He stopped at the girl's sharp intake of breath. Her face was paler than Mel's wings. What had he said? He tried to read the girl's soul, but she'd locked it up tighter than a drum.

Mel stepped between them and grabbed the girl's arm. She murmured something in a low voice, but Luce couldn't make out more than a word or two of it. The dangerous look in Mel's eyes told him not to say another word. It was Japan all over again.

Mel's hand curled around his arm instead — she'd let go of the girl and a slight jerk of her head indicated they should head down the stairs away from the strange girl. "My love?"

Luce nodded and departed with her. "I'm sorry," he whispered.

Mel looked mischievous. "Honestly, Luce, I'm beginning to think chaining you to the bed wasn't such a bad idea after all."

He grinned. If that's what she wanted, Hell, so did he. "Of course it's not a bad idea. I suggested it." A dangerous thought occurred to him. "But it only works if you're there with me. If you chain me up alone and leave me there while you go sightseeing without me, it's the worst idea I've ever heard."

She laughed gently. "I agree. I'm not sure I could look the landlord in the eye again if he walked in and found you." She blushed.

"Can you tell me why you wanted me to read souls up there? And what that girl is?" Luce hoped his voice was quiet enough not to carry to the strange girl.

Mel bit her lip. "She's a twenty-four-year-old intern doctor. When she was seventeen, she was abducted and spent almost a month being tortured like one of the souls in Lili's level of Hell. She survived because that man she was with helped her kill her abductors." She closed her eyes. "If I hadn't stepped between you, she was going to gut you with a hunting knife she keeps up her sleeve. You said something that made her think you knew what had happened to her and in her mind that marked you as one of her abductors."

"So that explains the soldier. Did they fall in love in Iraq or whatever and he brought her over here, where it's safe?"

Mel's eyes widened. "Iraq? Luce, she was abducted right outside the HELL Corporation offices on the Terrace and held in a place not far from where we're staying now. And he's no soldier – he's a security guard at the Perth Arena."

"Outside our building?" Luce sucked in a breath. "Were any of our staff involved?"

Mel shook her head. "No, they were all

human, if you can call them that. I'm sure you can find their souls in Hell, if you want more details. Well, unless any of them are still alive."

"I thought she was a terrorist," Luce admitted. "I figured you wanted me to stop her from doing whatever she had planned."

"I wouldn't put you in danger like that, Luce. I only wanted to know how well you could read souls from a distance. Next time, I'll stick to the more saintly sort."

Twenty-three

They were the first to reach the lower landing, so Luce pulled Mel to one of the few benches below the rocky overhang that wasn't wet. "Are you all right?" he asked, looking worried.

"Why wouldn't I be?" Mel lifted his hand, which was clamped around hers, to her lips for a light kiss. "It's my soul that's tired, not my body. A few flights of stairs aren't going to kill me, though you've been very conscientious in trying to heal me at every opportunity. It's very sweet of you, my love."

Why wasn't he more surprised? "So you did notice. I thought when you didn't stop me…" He eyed her laughing smile. "Right. Yeah. I should have known. Just that you've been drifting off to sleep so easily that I figured that was one of the symptoms of…whatever's ailing you."

"I've been watching you," she began, sounding almost timid. Luce felt his dread build – of course she was watching him for signs of his demonic nature reasserting itself. Not even Mel believed he was properly redeemed yet. Especially not after his lapse in Japan with the horrible Han woman. "And it's easier to focus on your soul when mine isn't engaged in maintaining my body. Sleep allows me to give your soul my full attention and you definitely deserve it, my love." She wasn't smiling – why wasn't she smiling?

"What have I done wrong?" he blurted out, not wanting to know and dying to, all at the same time.

She hesitated, seeming as reluctant to tell him as he was to hear it. "The way you heal me. It's…different, slower than the way I heal, and I thought perhaps if I watched you more closely, I'd work out why and I'd be able to help you." He sighed and her eyes widened. "No, I'm sorry, don't take it the wrong way. I just wanted to help you and I thought…oh, never mind. I was wrong."

Luce snorted. Mel was never wrong.

"You said you were a healer before, when you were in Heaven. Before the Heavenly Battle. And you told me you only healed angels, but I never understood what that meant until I saw you heal me. When you did it in Patrick's flat, I felt the air currents change the moment you started. I dismissed it as just his draughty old building, but then I felt the same thing in your penthouse and again here. Whatever it was, you were responsible. So I watched and tried to understand." She swallowed. "I'm sorry. I really thought you were doing something wrong, something I'd need to help you fix, but it wasn't until last night that I understood. You've been drawing energy from everything surrounding you — especially the kinetic energy from the air. Your soul concentrates it somehow and then directs that flow into mine. Not my body, which is what I initially thought. You're channelling the energy in the room into my soul." There was wonder in her eyes. Not since the night she'd transformed him from demon to angel had she looked at him quite like that.

"How –" Luce began, but it sounded hoarse. He coughed and tried again. "How am I supposed to heal you?"

Mel shook her head, a strange negative when her shining eyes shouted the opposite. She wet her lips. "I…I heal by taking the energy from my soul, summoning the atoms you need to heal…or to be clothed…and transferring these to you. It's a rapid, intimate exchange that flows easily between us because of how much I love you and how willing I am to give it to you. What you do…is slow, because it must be, but it's not limited by you. You could take the energy from a gust of wind and use it to restore a soul…or assemble a diamond from the carbon in charcoal…or transform yourself. Or you could take the energy from an explosion to protect everyone in the blast radius. And you can do this without depleting your soul's own energy. You're a remarkable angel, Luce. No one else can do what you can."

He stared at her, unable to close his mouth. She thought HE was doing something wonderful? That had to be a first. He had to be doing it wrong, that was all. Tonight, when they were alone in their apartment, he'd ask her to show him how to do it properly.

"No, Luce. I've been learning from you. Last night, feeling the tingle of energy flowing from you deep into me, restoring me more every moment. Oh my. It was better than…better than…" She blushed furiously. "And you know you're good, Luce, but what you did last night was incredible."

Surely she was joking. "But…last night I fell asleep. So did you. I don't understand how —"

"Shhh." Mel jerked her head at the humans making their way down the last flight of stairs to their landing.

Reluctantly, Luce shut up. For the moment. As soon as they got to the car, he was going to ask her how he'd managed to be incredible while sending them both to sleep, so he could do it again when he was awake, alert and watching her reaction.

Twenty-four

"There. That looks like everyone, so let's get started," the green-shirted, female ranger announced. She beamed around and Luce took stock of the other humans on the tour. The killer couple were nowhere in sight. Good. He didn't want to spill his blood into this cave pool like he had the one in Hell's bathroom. It would take years for the water to replenish naturally before he'd want to wash in it again. If ever.

He tuned out of the woman's rehearsed

briefing. Hell, what use was a safety briefing to him? He'd lived in the caves of Hell for millennia. He knew it hurt if you bumped your head on a stalactite. It's not like he'd be flying up around the ceiling.

Finally, she unlocked a gate and ushered them down the second half of the stairs – into the dark, by the look of things. Luce let everyone else go first, then he brought up the rear behind Mel. He didn't need to hear the running commentary. Mel could probably give him a far more informative tour if he had any questions – like what colour a fossil's fur was in life. Or if there were any of those clawed crayfish things in the lake.

He ducked under an overhanging rock and followed Mel deeper. Grey, weathered limestone gave way to cream as his eyes adjusted to the dim lighting. A spotlit boardwalk led them further into the depths, suspended over what looked like a deep pit. Luce looked closer and realised he wasn't looking at a pit at all, but dark water reflecting the ceiling above.

He whooped in triumph. Lake Cave was

true to its name and finally something had gone right today.

He became aware of seven pairs of human eyes and one amused angel staring at him.

"I take it this cave is the right one, my love," Mel said softly.

Someone sniggered in the dark.

"Yes," Luce replied, holding his head high. "Much better than Mammoth Cave."

While the tour guide waxed lyrical about how caves were created, her voice may as well have been water dripping on a stone to Luce. He surveyed the lake and the stalactites above it, before his attention landed firmly on the column that was both wider and taller than he was. It appeared to end on a little limestone island in the lake, until he looked closer. No, not in the lake – floating in mid-air, at least a foot above it.

Mel's hand tugged at his, so Luce plodded along the boardwalk, his eyes still on the column. From the other side, the column beside it presented a far more interesting view. "Look, that must be Satan's Little Finger, Luce."

"It doesn't look like anyone's finger to me," he responded, grinning at the man-sized, bulbous rock cock.

"Shhh," she said again, drawing Luce's attention to the only child in the tour group. The girl's eyes were firmly fixed on Luce and the woman holding the girl's hand – presumably her mother – shot a suspicious glance in his direction.

He sighed and fell silent.

The tour guide beckoned them further along and Mel led him to the end of the boardwalk, a row of benches and a stone beach that sloped gently into the lake. She started talking about cave formations again, flicking various coloured lights on to highlight the features as she described them.

Mel paid polite attention, but Luce didn't have the patience for a geology lesson and light show. He'd been good for long enough.

The black buttons of his polo shirt were hard to see in the dark, but he managed to undo them by touch before pulling the shirt off entirely. He kicked off his shoes and socks, leaving them in a jumbled pile on the seat.

Lastly, he dropped his pants.

He glanced back to find out why the tour guide had fallen silent.

All human eyes were on him again, while Mel was staring fixedly at her shoes and smothering laughter. No, not all the humans. The girl's father had his hands over his daughter's eyes, as if he was afraid she'd be corrupted just by looking at him.

"What? Aren't you dying to take a dip in water this pure, too? To swim under that floating rock ledge to make sure it's not an illusion?" A sudden thought occurred to him and he stepped out of his pants and strode to the water's edge to dip his toes in. "Hell, it's cold. Is the whole lake that cold? Is that why no one else is getting ready to swim?"

"You can't go swimming in the lake and definitely not like that. It's home to unique stygofauna found nowhere else on Earth." The ranger suddenly stood beside Luce, glaring up at him. "Get away from the water before you do any more damage." She looked like she was ready to drag him bodily away from the edge.

Luce grinned, daring her to try it. The

minute she touched him, he'd...

"I'm sorry, you'll have to forgive us," Mel's gentle voice said. "We've been exploring the Nullarbor caves, which are nowhere near as accessible and well-maintained as this one. When fewer people can get to them, there's far more freedom for those of us who do." She pressed his pants against his groin. "We've been so used to swimming in the remote caves that we thought we'd have the opportunity to do that in this one, too. I'm sorry for the misunderstanding." She took Luce's arm and dropped her voice to a carrying whisper. "Please, my love, put your clothes back on or I'll be too busy staring at you to listen to the rest of the tour. And she said the cold water has something called gilgies in it – crayfish things with claws."

Grumpily, Luce pulled his pants back on and allowed her to pull him back to the bench, where he sat and glowered until the tour guide led the way outside again. To make matters worse, one of his shoes had been under a ceiling drip, so now his left sock was all soggy.

Daylight would be a relief after the

disappointing cave, he decided, looking up the first flight of stairs. Then he recalled just how many stairs they'd climbed down to reach the cave — the same stairs he was about to ascend. One hundred? Two? More?

"Only five hundred and eighteen stairs to the top!" the ranger announced with a forced smile, taking a swig from her water bottle. She wasn't going up them — she was staying for the next tour group, Luce realised.

Grumbling under his breath, he followed Mel up to the surface. Could this accursed day get any worse?

Twenty-five

Luce could tell Mel was struggling by about halfway up. She'd slowed right down and her knuckles were white as she clutched the hand rails. When she paused, he moved to stand right behind her, his mouth level with her ear. "I'll carry you the rest of the way if you want."

"I walked into and out of Hell just fine. I'm sure I can make my way out of this cave. They're just stairs, after all. Just...so many of them." He felt her deep sigh as much as he heard it. "What do you have in mind for the rest of the afternoon? Please don't say another cave or a hike."

"Wine tasting is what I'd planned," Luce began uncertainly, "but if you want to give it a miss and head home to rest, we'll do it."

Mel's second sigh sounded happier. "I want both. Let's go choose a lovely bottle of red to take home to relax with. Can we eat in tonight, like we did last night? We still have enough of those dumplings to feed a small army and I didn't even cook the steamed pork buns." She started up the stairs again. "If I'm going to get into the pork buns after that lunch we had, I need all the exercise I can get."

Luce had some ideas for exercise they could do together, but he kept his mouth shut as he indulged his imagination.

When they reached the top, Mel paused to give him a pointed look. "I don't think we could do all you have in mind in one night, but we'll see," she said with a wink before she led the way to the car.

His mind-reading angel. Luce snorted and followed her.

In the car, he leaned across her and pulled

out the map he'd picked up from the tourist centre. "Luce Iblis, chauffeur, at your service, my lady. Tell me where to go."

Mel laughed. "The best chauffeur I ever had, just like you promised."

He glanced behind him. "I promised you a good time in the back seat, too. The offer still stands."

Once again, Mel left him hanging. "Mmm, so many wineries. Maybe…ooh, this is the one with the beautiful gardens. The first time we shared dinner together, we had a delicious bottle of white from here. Maybe they have nice reds, too."

Luce tilted his head to try and make out the name obscured by her finger. "What's the place called?"

"Lay-win? Loo-win? Leeuwin, anyway."

Luce traced the route on the map and nodded. The car's engine purred into life and they headed back onto Caves Road.

Mel scanned the signs as eagerly as he did, but they both spotted the correct one at the same time. "There!"

Luce turned into the side street and the

search began anew for the next sign pointing the way. Short of flashing neon lights, the place couldn't be more clearly marked. A sealed road wound between grassy paddocks that were bordered by low fences and powerful floodlights. The gum trees lining the ridge were like strange sentinels in the manicured fields. Where were the grape vines? Or the huge industrial plant needed to turn grapes so bad they became good again? The road curved down and ended abruptly in a car park. He couldn't see the buildings through the gardens, either, though a paved path led to some steps.

Mel seemed just as mystified, but the eagerness in her eyes said she was enjoying the experience. Movement on the sloping lawns caught his eye and he squinted at the odd lumps on the otherwise velvet grass.

"Oh, look, Luce, more ring-necks," Mel said, pointing at the lumps. One of them raised its head and revealed that it was indeed a bird and not part of the grass at all. Melodious bird laughter carried on the breeze from the trees at the bottom of the hill and all five camouflaged birds raised their heads to answer the ringing call before taking flight to join them. Mel cuddled closer to him, still smiling as they walked arm in arm along the path to the building hidden behind the trees and huge hedges.

A sign for the toilets caught Mel's eye next and she excused herself to make use of the facilities. So Luce walked alone into the winery and took a seat on a convenient couch by the flickering fire.

When Mel eventually entered the room, she glanced around but didn't seem to see him. Luce watched her approach the bar with an uncertain smile on her face.

"Tasting today?" the girl behind the bar asked, flipping a wine glass onto the polished jarrah at Mel's nod. "What do you like?"

Milkshakes. Chocolate. Red wine. Tea. Those bloody green parrots that kept laughing at him. Those big, pink, star-shaped flowers with the strong smell. He should get some flowers for her. Maybe that would make her smile, and make up for the mess he'd made of the day. He slipped outside and called Mephi.

"Good afternoon, Mr Iblis."

"Mephi, do you remember last Valentine's Day, when I got flowers for Mel?"

"Yes, Mr Iblis. You purchased some sort of orchids, I remember. They were beautiful." Did he catch a note of approval in her voice?

"I need more flowers for her, but something different this time. She had…someone else sent her pink flowers. They smelled. They were the cheapest flowers in the florist I went to, but she insisted they had an alluring scent and whoever bought them knew they were her favourite. Do you know what they were?" He could hear his own desperation, but he didn't care.

"I…I'm not sure I remember, Mr Iblis."

"Ask someone on Reception or that snippy archangel she worked with. Someone must have seen them when they were delivered. Someone has to remember!"

"One moment, Mr Iblis." Mephi's calm voice was replaced by piano music. On hold. Oh, could his day get worse? After the fifth rendition of the same tune, Mephi rescued him. "I spoke to Merih. He said she only had roses and orchids. They stayed by her desk all week."

Luce gritted his teeth. "No, she had pink flowers on the day. I saw her leave with them. They had…the paper around them had a sticker with the logo from the plaza florist. Ask them what pink flowers they sold on Valentine's Day that smelled."

"Yes, Mr Iblis."

He ground his teeth through a tortuous seven renditions of the same dull song before it ended.

"Mr Iblis, the only scented flowers she sold were called Asiatic liliums. A young woman came in and bought them all."

Mel had a female admirer? So she'd enchanted not just the male demons but the female ones, too? Or were they from an angel?

"She said the young woman bought some chocolates, too. Both the flowers and the chocolates were ordered by mistake and she had no space in the cool room for them, so she was at a loss for what to do with them when the young woman walked in, bought the lot and solved all her problems for the day. Like an angel, she said she was."

Not a demon. Definitely an angel. But who?

Luce remembered the archangel who'd seized a handful of Mel's chocolates – the same one who'd told him to go to Hell instead of taking Mel on holiday. The one who'd dragged Mel away from him at the office Christmas picnic.

Damn it. When he got home, he'd hunt her down and tell her to leave him and Mel alone.

But for now…"Mephi, find somewhere in Margaret River or nearby who has them and have a huge bunch delivered to our accommodation. Today if you can, but tomorrow at the latest. With a vase, because I'm not sure our apartment has one. And a card." He swallowed, not wanting to say the words aloud.

"What would you like written on the card, Mr Iblis?"

He had to. If there wasn't a card, she might think the flowers were from that angel instead of him. His voice died to a whisper. "For my sweet angel. Love Luce."

To his shock, Mephi didn't laugh – or sound horrified by his weakness. In fact, her voice softened. "I'll see to it, Mr Iblis."

He breathed a sigh of relief and returned to his seat by the fire, where he could watch his sweet angel lose herself in the smell and taste of each savoured sip.

Twenty-Six

"Would you like to try the Art Series Riesling or would you like to move straight to the reds?" the girl behind the bar asked, glancing at the bottles in her hands.

Mel requested the reds before drinking deeply from her glass of water. While the white wines had all demonstrated complex flavours culminating in a smooth finish, none had been to her taste. Perhaps it was the soils here – or the years, or the selection…she sighed. She was looking for the white she'd shared with

Luce, but she couldn't remember any more than the fact that the wine had been from here. Her heart had been too full of sorrow at saying goodbye. But none of these tasted right – plus she wanted a bottle of red to share with him tonight, not white.

Nodding to the girl's description of the shiraz in her glass, Mel swirled the liquid around, inhaling deeply. Mulberries. Red currants. And a touch of the eucalypts that must grow near the grapevines. She sipped with her eyes closed, holding the wine in her mouth, before lifting her chin to allow it to trickle down her throat as she swallowed. The pepper and oak burned her throat on the way down. No. This one was too spicy for her taste. She tipped the contents of her glass into the spittoon and rinsed both the glass and her mouth liberally with water. A waiter whose muscled arms bulged in his black sleeves said something quietly to the girl, who nodded gravely.

"Next is the Art Series Shiraz…" The girl poured and lowered her voice. "I don't mean to alarm you, but Serge says there's a man who hasn't stopped staring at you since you came in and he looks…dangerous. He said the man went outside to make a phone call, but he kept looking back inside. He's on the sofa by the fire now and he's looking at you like…like you killed his whole family and today he'll have his vengeance, Serge says."

Oh, not the security guard from the caves. She'd only touched his girlfriend – not hurt her. But if she'd mentioned Luce frightening her, Mel would need to somehow send him away before he spotted Luce. Mel started to turn and the alarmed girl grabbed her arm.

"No! Please…if you look at him, he might come over here and even Serge says he looks scary. When you're finished tasting, Serge offered to walk you out to your car. He's a waiter, but he's learning to be a personal trainer and he…well, he's…you know." The girl blushed as she curled her bicep in imitation of Serge's.

Intrigued, Mel went through the motions of sampling the remaining reds, but now she knew she was under scrutiny, it was an effort to swallow a thing, let alone taste the nuances of the well-aged wines. Sighing, she thanked the girl and turned to go.

"Wait. He's still staring at you. I'll distract him and as soon as he's looking the other way, you sneak out with Serge."

Staring sounded more like Luce than the security guard, whose scrutiny would surely be more covert. Mel was dying to turn and see if her audience really was Luce, but if he wasn't and the man intended to harm her, best if she was outside with fewer witnesses. She watched the girl box up several expensive bottles of wine. The girl winked and walked around the bar, swinging the box at her side.

"Here you are, sir. That will be one hundred and eighty-three dollars," she heard the girl say.

"Now!" Serge hissed, placing an arm lightly around Mel so he could propel her faster out of the cellar door. Together, they hurried down the steps. "Which is your car?" he asked, scanning the car park.

Mel pointed at Luce's black Jaguar. "That one. But I don't have the keys — my partner does. And I haven't seen him since we arrived."

Luce exploded through a shrub. "Mel? Are you all right? You ran out and I thought –"

Serge edged forward, placing himself between Mel and Luce. Mel recognised it as a gallant attempt to protect her, but one that would only end badly for the personal trainer-in-training.

"I wondered why you didn't join me for tasting, my love," she said, marching to Luce's side, where she claimed a kiss.

He chuckled. "Watching you abandon yourself to each taste was way better than drinking the stuff myself. The way you lift your closed eyes to Heaven as you lose yourself in your own private world of sensation…bloody Hell, I wanted to take you up against that bar, right then and there, and to Hell with anyone watching." Evidently Luce was the staff's mystery man – watching her with an intensity that they'd found frightening.

Mel couldn't help blushing. She turned to the confused waiter. "Thank you for walking me to my car. With my partner here, I'm sure I'll be fine now. Please…please tell your friend that I'm thankful for her kindness. And yours."

Mel's eyes followed the man back inside, but Luce's gaze was firmly fixed on her. As they climbed into his car, he asked, "Nothing you liked in there? Fair enough. Where to next?"

Mel glanced at the map and named a winery she'd never heard of that was along their route home. She hoped they'd have something suitable.

Fifteen minutes later, Luce pulled into the parking lot of the next winery.

So there'd be no misunderstandings here, Mel kept a firm hand on his arm. She didn't want anyone making the same mistake again. There was nothing wrong with the way Luce stared at her, because they were together and…

She almost missed her mouth with the wineglass. Had he truly been staring that intently at her in the previous place? Like he was breathless with lust from just looking at her? She felt naked, exposed, as if he'd caught her doing something incredibly personal in public. What was she doing that he found so erotic?

"So which ones did you like best?" the man

at the tasting bar asked.

Mel swallowed the last of the dessert wine and stared at the list of wines she'd drunk, but couldn't remember the taste of a single one. "I...I don't know," she said softly, staring at the floor to hide her flushing cheeks.

Luce's arm snaked around her waist. "Well, if none of these are your favourite, we'll try somewhere else." He nodded his thanks at the man and led Mel outside. She exhaled gratefully as the stiff breeze cooled her cheeks.

The next winery was no better – nor the next, though they stopped at a few places along the way that sold food, too. The more she drank, the more Mel wanted to give in to the invitation in Luce's eyes, but the less she tasted of the wines she was supposed to be selecting. Where was the point in sampling them when she wasn't really focussing on the wines at all? Finally, she said, "I'm tired, Luce. Please...can we just go home?"

She couldn't meet his hurt eyes as he asked, "Home? You mean the loft here, my apartment in Perth or your little house?" The forlorn note in his voice tugged at her heart.

"I meant the loft. Where it's just us."

"Sure." He grinned and led the way back to the car.

Mel drowsed as he drove, stroking his thigh absently. Surely he wasn't tensing up under her touch. Did he think she'd hurt him? Or was it her weakness – he didn't want her starting something he didn't think they could finish, because her soul was still exhausted? She'd seen how her strength turned him on – perhaps her vulnerability did the opposite. In her heart, she knew no one could help her recover like Luce could – but he had to be willing. Or it could be too soon.

She sighed deeply and watched the modern terracotta building swing into sight behind the trees. Fumbling around in the footwell for her purchases, she realised she'd bought fruit, vegetables, cheese and other produce, but not the bottle of wine they were looking for. Mel glanced at her watch. The cellar door downstairs closed in fifteen minutes – surely she could find something there. Only…not if she was feeling self-conscious as her thoughts drifted to far more pleasurable things than wine.

Luce opened her car door for her and leaned in to take her bundles from her, or so she thought. Instead, he seized her – oranges, jam, venison and all – swinging her easily into his arms to carry up the stairs.

Mel cried out as her leg muscle seized in an agonising spasm. The combination of so many stairs and then sitting too long, surely.

"Oh God, what is it? Did I hurt you?" The surrounding temperature dropped five degrees as Luce summoned the energy to heal whatever was wrong.

Mel glanced around. They weren't alone in the car park – some wine tasters were loading their car. Well, they had been until she'd yelped. Now they were standing by their car and looking worried, as if they wondered whether they should intervene. "No, just…just put me down. A muscle cramp, that's all. I should walk it off."

The pain eased as her feet hit the gravel. She felt Luce pry her purchases from her arms before she opened her eyes and took a cautious step. Better.

"There's no hurry," Luce said softly, concern creasing his features.

"How about you take everything upstairs and make a start on dinner? I'll get us a bottle of wine and then I'll be right up to help you." Mel slowly made her way to the stone steps. Only three, she told herself as she clamped her mouth shut to tackle them. Mildly painful, but not unbearable. When they reached the grass at the top, she released Luce's arm and kissed him lightly. "Trust me. I promise I won't get the chili one."

That did it. Of course he trusted her and he knew his reluctance would look like distrust. Mel watched Luce climb the stairs and he looked like he was just as unaccustomed to today's climbing marathon as she was. She couldn't wait to stroke the tension out of those muscles in the spa.

But first…the wine.

Twenty-Seven

The door squeaked open and Mel smiled at Greg, for they were alone. He looked appraisingly at her, but he waited until she stood at the tasting bar before he broke the silence.

"Is everything all right upstairs?"

Oh, cleverly done, Mel thought. It was both an invitation to ask for fresh towels or spill her troubles. She intended to do both.

"Mmm, everything upstairs is wonderful." She let her bliss infuse her voice. "We might need fresh towels tomorrow, though. They dry so slowly in this weather and with the spa, we do use a few." She laughed gently. "And there's the small matter of a bottle of wine for tonight. We've been all over the place, tasting every red on offer, but I couldn't find something suitable for tonight. I really wanted something special."

He set a tasting glass on the bar beside her. "I have two new ones we just bottled this week – I only brought them up here this afternoon. They won't go on sale until tomorrow, when I bring some more cases up, but I could spare you a bottle or two of each tonight, if you like them."

Mel agreed and watched the liquid cascade into her glass.

She took her time tasting these, listening to the vintner's descriptions of each bottle's history. One tingled on her tongue and she reached for her glass again, just to make sure she'd tasted right. "Raspberries," she breathed. What was it about raspberries that made even the hint of the taste of them an aphrodisiac?

Greg grinned. "You like that one?"

"Oh yes. I think I'd like two…no, make it

three. Three bottles for now, please, and a case in the morning." She winked. "But not too early. I hope you don't intend to stay back late tonight."

He produced three bottles, boxed them up for her, and processed her payment.

Mel sighed happily as she hugged the box to her chest.

"Enjoy your evening," he drawled with a knowing grin.

Mel thought of Luce waiting for her upstairs. "Oh, I will."

Twenty-eight

"Ohhh, that feels good," Mel groaned as blissful heat engulfed her.

Across the apartment, Luce drove all his guilt into the bottle opener, grinding it into the cork. It was his fault her legs were aching and she wouldn't let him heal her. He should never have taken her to the cave – it didn't matter how pretty the underground lake was. Hell, it wasn't as if they'd been allowed to swim in it, like the one back in his lair in the depths of Hell. All that wine tasting and she'd only liked one bottle of wine – one! – and they'd wasted all afternoon sniffing, sipping, swirling, swallowing and spitting. The shiraz in his hands was from the cellar door downstairs, or they'd have had nothing to drink tonight.

"I'm sorry," he found himself saying, "so sorry for stuffing up today. I couldn't do anything right. I'll make it up to you tomorrow, I swear. We can go out for breakfast and the rest of the day is up to you – whatever you want to do. Seeing as I'm hopeless at planning activities, you choose. I'm so sorry, Mel."

"Luce, come here," she said softly.

Hesitantly, he crossed the floor until he stood directly behind her on the tiles by the spa. The bubbles hid her body and her face was turned away from him. He'd earned it, he knew. He didn't deserve her attention. What a monumental mess he'd made of what was supposed to be a relaxing holiday for her.

She tilted her head back, so he could see her sweet smile and sympathetic eyes. "No. Come join me in the spa, my love. No clothes needed – though it would be nice if you brought the wine."

Three strides carried him back to the table. He gathered up the bottle and glasses and presented them to Mel. She placed the glasses carefully on the tiled ledge by the window and proceeded to pour the wine. Lifting a filled glass to her lips, she turned to face Luce. Her breasts floated tantalisingly among the bubbles. "Please join me."

Luce's mouth was dry. He couldn't refuse. He lifted his leg over the edge of the spa and realised he was still dressed. Mumbling an apology, he fumbled with his shirt buttons, wishing he could undo them faster. After what seemed like forever, he managed to pull off his polo shirt. Under Mel's admiring gaze, he unbuttoned his pants. "You want me to take it all off?"

"Yes, I do, my love."

He managed a wicked grin as he slipped his hand into his pants. "You know I have a loaded weapon in here. You sure you want me to let the safety off?" Hell, he didn't sound anywhere near as confident as he should have. She was going to laugh – turn cold – shoot him down…

"I have seen it all before, Luce, and as recently as this morning, but if it makes you feel better, I can turn around and close my eyes while you get in. The bubbles should cover plenty if you're feeling a bit shy."

"No," he breathed. He dropped his trousers and clambered into the tub. "Hell, it's hot!" Luce lowered himself gingerly into the steaming water.

Mel offered, "I can add some cold water if you need it. The heat helps sore muscles relax."

Luce could feel the hot water working its magic on his calves already. "I'm good. I'm used to heat, being a demon for so long and all. Besides, you need it more than I do. You're not used to…I'm so stupid. I'm sorry about today, Mel. Is there anything I can do to make it up to you to make a messed-up day not so bad?"

She reached for the wineglasses and held them high above the bubbles as she slid around the tub to sit beside him. "First, have a sip of the best red I've tasted all day."

Luce took a glass from her and drank.

Grudgingly, he agreed that she was right about the wine. "What else? I'd do anything for you, Mel."

Her foot stroked the length of his leg, from his thigh to his toes and back again. "Let me tell you about the best day I've had this year. I woke up in bed with the man I love. Together, we watched the sun rise over the lake as we shared breakfast. Some time later, we climbed into his luxury car and drove down country roads between green paddocks and swathes of state forest full of towering trees. We stopped at a few places along the way to taste wine and fresh produce, and we even bought some of it to enjoy later. Along with treating me to a decadent lunch, he took me on tours of two beautiful caves, where the underground lakes and streams were full of reflections – just like the one he'd shown me once before, but circumstances hadn't allowed us to enjoy together. After the caves, he treated me to a magnificent dinner in our little loft studio. I was a little distracted, because all I could think about was sharing a big bath of hot water with the man I love – and the spa inside met my needs perfectly. And you're asking if you can make my day better? I can only think of one thing that could take my blissful day and make it perfect."

His breathing was ragged. Her hands had started stroking the rest of his body, and she wasn't shy. "Name it, Melody, and it's yours."

She smiled as she took a slow mouthful of wine, then licked her lips before she said, "Make love to me in the water, Luce. The pleasurable end to the perfect day you've given me." She set her glass on the ledge and leaned back, her loving eyes fixed on him.

Luce ran a tentative hand up her leg, soothing away any aches that the hot water hadn't taken away, before stroking away the pain from her other leg. He felt her legs part beneath his fingers and he hesitated. "Are you sure? What do you want me to do? How…how do you want to do this?" His mouth felt dry with desire, but there was no way in Hell he was going to make this any less than perfect for her. He might have slept with a hundred…a thousand…or a hundred thousand women before her, but they were all practice so he'd know how to please his precious angel.

"I want my sexy devil to drive. Do what you do best, my love."

Twenty-nine

"Thank you, Luce, for everything," she said sleepily, snuggling up to him in bed afterwards.

Luce was sated and exhausted, his body still buzzing from their incredible lovemaking. "I don't deserve you. When I dreamed about all the things I wanted to do with you and to you, I never thought any of those dreams would come true. But now –"

"Demons dream?" Mel asked, suddenly staring at him.

His cheeks heated as they flushed. "Not

dream, not really," he muttered. "More like daydreams. Fantasies. When those dark souls in Hell wrap around your soul, there's no getting out. No leaving your body for anything, except to join them in terrorising other souls. Trapped in your own head, sometimes it's pleasant to imagine how good life could be, if circumstances were different. Sometimes, I just used my body's down-time to plan my next attempt to take over the world, telling myself that maybe the domination of Earth wasn't as impossible a goal as I'd thought. Maybe this time, I'd get closer…" He clenched his teeth, trying to block out all the painful memories.

Her gentle hands stroked them away. "You can't get much closer than you are now, my love. And I'm sorry if I caused you grief. I was just surprised, is all. I mean, angels don't dream, but humans do, and I know so little about demons that I wondered. I wanted to ask you what it was like."

"I know. It's all right." Luce pulled her closer, praying that her skin against his would be enough to keep the darkness at bay. "What do you do at night, while your body slumbers in my willing arms? Do you watch me as I watch you?"

Mel hesitated before she said, "When you're not with me and I miss you, yes, sometimes I leave my body and travel to where you are so I can see you. Once when you were in New York…and once more when I was in Japan without you. It's not an indulgence I permit myself often. Most nights, I walk the paths of the future, trying to determine the correct course of action to yield optimal results. Or I visit mortals who hold the key to these desirable futures, as their decisions are the nodes separating the present from what could be. I speak to them in their dreams and give them insights into probable futures, in the hope that I can persuade them to make a beneficial decision. Sometimes, I even help them with other significant parts of their lives and responsibilities, if they desire my assistance."

Like the Hans in Korea. "What about tonight? When we're supposed to be on holiday, with no work to do, will you desert me as we sleep so that you can continue working yourself far too hard? While I thought you were peacefully resting last night, were you still trying to solve the world's problems?"

Mel's lips were warm as she kissed his chest. "No, my love. Last night I watched you healing me and finally understood how you managed it. But the other nights here…on our first night, I sensed an owl and I spent most of the nights this week just watching the night wildlife and the stars, as they lived their hidden lives in the darkness outside this place. I lost count of the number of kangaroos that came past."

Oh God, was that her tongue rasping across his nipple? So that's why men have nipples. So that Mel could…Luce's mouth went dry. "Can I…may I join you in your stargazing tonight, if you're going to do the same thing? If you don't mind having company, that is. I'll need your help, though. I've never left my body to travel the way you do. As a demon, I couldn't, and when I was an angel, I never spent enough time in a human body to experience sleep. I wouldn't know how…" He trailed off as he saw Mel's eyes widening with shock.

She swallowed several times, as if her mouth was as dry as his. "I'm so sorry, Luce. Some mentor I am. I never thought to ask you and I had no idea you didn't know how. I'll share the stars with you until sunrise and the start of a new day." Mel tilted her head up and gave Luce a lingering kiss. "Sleep, my love. I can't wait to steal your soul." She settled against his chest once more, releasing a deep sigh that seemed to relax her whole body as she exhaled.

Luce closed his eyes, trying to empty his mind enough to put his brain to sleep. Steal his soul? It was already hers. She couldn't steal something she owned so completely. He felt his lips lift in a smile before he drifted into slumber.

Thirty

"Can you hear me, my love?" Mel's voice held far more power without a human body to restrain it. "Lucifer, light of the morning, can you feel me?"

Warmth touched his soul, spreading to envelope him completely. The dawn of the first perfect morning in Heaven – or Mel's soul embracing him. No other sensation his soul knew could be as blissful as this. He didn't want to break the moment. "I love you."

Her soul hummed with laughter. "And I

love you, but you're not going to see any stars unless you free your soul from that body. I can drag you out, but it's best if you do it yourself, so you know how to."

"You can rip my soul from my body?" Luce didn't remember being able to do that as an angel. Hell, it was a damn good thing demons couldn't do it.

"There's a reason demons are trapped in their bodies. Yes, your every thought is open to me as if you'd spoken it. Any angel who works as an escort must learn to do it, for when a soul won't leave a corpse and needs that extra push." She hummed with laughter again. "Luce, is that a challenge?"

It was Luce's turn to laugh. "I'll make it clearer, then. Come claim my arse and I'm all yours."

He sensed her confusion. "I thought you'd want to do it yourself, but you have a strong desire for some sort of violence from me," she said. "Luce, I'm not…"

"I haven't been out of this body for millennia, and even the thought of you using that kind of power over me does things to my libido you wouldn't believe. Please, take me to the stars, Melody."

Luce felt her mirth as she seemed to wrap tighter around him, forming a blissful bubble with him on the inside. Heaven. No, better than Heaven. Secure in her embrace, he dared to look around. Everything was dark, moving past so fast it was difficult to recognise anything. The only constant was the stars, which were above…no, around…no…on all sides except underneath, which looked like…"Mel, why have we left the Earth's atmosphere?"

"I'm giving you the stars, my love, or at least the only one I can give you tonight. Have you ever seen a solar tempest up close before?"

Luce looked up. The Earth might be receding fast, but the huge white sphere loomed larger by the second. He'd been free of his body for less than ten minutes, and Mel was about to fly him into the sun.

Thirty-one

He'd never seen anything like it. It was like watching ocean waves swelling in a storm, except these were far more fluid and on a much larger scale. Maybe like liquid mist. Only mist on Earth could never be this powerful. Cyclonic clouds, maybe, as they churned the ocean into a waterspout…

"Isn't it gorgeous? So much raw power is pretty awesome."

Luce did a double-take at the sound of a voice that wasn't Mel's. "Who in Hell are you and what are you doing out in the vacuum of space?"

"Avoiding arrogance like yours. Lady Muriel, did he promise you eternal servitude for bringing him out here? If not, you deserve it."

Mel hummed with laughter while Luce looked for the unwelcome soul. Its energy signature was so close to that of the sun that he had to focus hard or lose it entirely.

"Saule, I take it you know Lucifer already? It must have been from a long time ago. I haven't seen you in this system for…ooh, must be going on five thousand years or more. I thought you were watching a black hole somewhere."

The soul hummed, as if she was laughing with Mel. "I was until Malakbel requested assistance keeping track of a stellar nursery over in the Sagittarius constellation. Belenos was bored with this stable star and dying to spend some more time with Malakbel, so he offered me everything under the sun to swap places with him. Give me a stable star with life-supporting planets like this one and I'm much happier, so I finally gave in and this star's mine for as long as I like. Or as long as Mr High and Mighty here continues to ignore all the Dynameis because we're beneath him. How'd you get him out of Heaven and all the way out here? Don't tell me he's finally taking an interest in the universe."

Mel's laughter had ceased. The muted glow flowing from her soul seemed like something more sombre. Sadness or mourning, perhaps. "You've been gone a long time. Luce has spent most of it in the world, as have I, but he's had the more difficult time of it. We're sharing our knowledge and I don't believe Luce has seen a solar tempest before. I wanted to share the experience with him." Luce felt her drift closer to him, a tendril of her being twining tighter around his. If she'd been in her human form, her body would be pressed along his side and her fingers would be gripping his hand.

"He doesn't share. He'll take everything you have to give and leave without a word of thanks, as he did to Meness. I expected to be reunited with my partner when I returned, only to discover that the Morning Star had somehow seduced him from the moon to Heaven, to fight for some hopeless cause. Now Meness is tainted, a demon condemned to Hell, and Lucifer? He doesn't look as if he's faced any consequences at all."

"Those who fought at my side fought for what they believed in and they chose their fate. I forced no one," Luce snapped. "I endured Hell for longer than any of the others, not that it's any of your business. And Meness? He's one of the few permanent staff in Level Eight. He favours the bolgia where he gets to transform damned souls into various creatures. From the moon to painful shapeshifting – it suits him."

Saule seethed, but Mel slipped between them. "I'm sorry for your loss. That Meness chose a path that led away from you is difficult to bear. It would break my heart to lose Luce as you have your partner."

"He doesn't deserve you, Lady Muriel."

Luce could see the conflict sapping Mel's strength, stealing away what little she had as if it was being swept into space by the solar wind. Of course he didn't deserve her. But she deserved every bit of help he could give her. Including healing. He focussed on pulling energy into himself, concentrating it so he could channel it into her. Without a body, it flowed so easily it felt effortless – just like it must have when he was an angel in Heaven. If this was so easy, then he could surely summon more power, perhaps even heal her more than he had before. Maybe, just maybe, he could truly start to repay her for everything she did for him. He drew in a deep beam of energy and…

"No – look out!"

Saule's warning came too late. The flare engulfed Mel and Luce completely, filling him with so much energy he felt like his soul was fizzing. The stream surged straight for Mel, the most powerful beam of energy he'd ever seen. And once it had started, he couldn't stop it. He'd sucked the flare into existence and it wouldn't subside until Mel had had her fill.

Mel screamed. It wasn't sound so much as pure energy slicing straight through him. He was hurting her. Oh God, he was hurting her and he couldn't stop. Mel. Oh God, Mel!

The beam seemed to hit a wall, reflecting back at him. Now he was screaming, too, just as Mel had. But it wasn't painful. He felt…euphoric. Energy flooded into him, filling the furthest reaches of his soul, until he felt like the most powerful being in the universe. Brimming with so much energy he might burst. Mel's scream still pierced him, but now he could sense the nuances surrounding it. Blissful, mind-blowing, joyful… "Mel, if I could give you an orgasm this good, I'd be the most legendary lover this universe has ever seen."

Laughter hummed. "You just did, my love."

The flare was finished and so was she. Melody Angel, Lady Muriel, the radiant, angelic soul at his side. He was glowing, but she was incandescent. If this was what she normally looked like, he'd never seen her on a good day, let alone her best.

"How did you do that?" Saule demanded. "That flare sent me halfway past Venus and it didn't budge you a bit. You both look like you…you drank it."

Mel twined herself tightly around Luce.

"Luce is a truly amazing angel and I'm delighted he chose to share that with me. Thank you, my love." There was a certain note of triumph in her tone. "Saule, I shall visit again when I can. Please, tell no one of this until I do."

Saule laughed, the humming slightly jittery as if her laughter was shaky. "No one would believe me. No angel can do that. And definitely no demon."

Luce stared at Mel. Healed. Finally, she was as strong as she was supposed to be. "I don't believe I did it."

"I do. You never cease to surprise me, my love. Saule is right – you don't deserve the exhausted angel you've been fighting to heal while I undo your efforts every day. You deserve a mentor at full strength." Her soul's light dimmed slightly, as if in mourning once more. "We should head back."

They both farewelled the sun's guardian angel and sped toward Earth and the little loft. Luce could have sworn they left a comet's tail streaming behind them as they streaked home.

Mel's soul sank into her body and Luce

hesitated for a moment. Surely his first night out of his body wouldn't be his last – Mel wouldn't leave him trapped in it for millennia again. He darted from air into flesh.

"He's not moving. I should have waited, shown him how to return to his body. Please don't leave me, Luce. I love you…I love you…I was right, you are still the angel you once were. Please don't leave me now. Thank you. I love you. Please don't reject me…" Mel's voice sounded clearly in his head as her lips touched his shoulder, his neck, his cheek and, finally, his lips.

Luce happily returned her passionate kiss, listening to her repeat the same litany in her audible thoughts. Finally, he broke the kiss to say, "Why in Hell would I leave you? I love you. I just sucked on the sun so you'd feel better. And you think I'd leave before I found out what my supercharged Melody can do?"

Her laughter was filled with joy. "You heard me! I was beginning to think you'd never be able to. What I can do…oh, I…I know what I'd like to do." The images in her mind were enough to make Luce blush almost as red as

Mel. "May I?"

May she? Hell, he'd beg for her to do half of what she just showed him. "Hell yes. Today's entirely up to you. From now until when we fall asleep tonight, you call the shots."

Her blush deepened. "Even in bed? Of the two of us, you're definitely the expert there. Far more experienced than I am."

He seized her and held her tight. "Especially in bed. You're my sweet angel, Melody, the very best." He groaned in bliss as she proved his point.

Thirty-two

"Now – out, so I can shave my legs," Mel ordered over the hissing shower stream.

"I can help," Luce offered eagerly, hanging his towel over the rail.

"I know, but I can do this. Can you hang that last load of laundry out on the balcony? With today's fine weather, it should dry before dark."

Luce hefted the basket of wet washing in one hand. "Winter in Western Australia and we're line-drying washing outside. You couldn't do this in London. Or Singapore. Middle of winter here and it's shaping up to be a perfect day."

"Another perfect day," Mel corrected. "Just like yesterday."

Luce didn't argue – he and Mel definitely disagreed on what a perfect day involved, but he didn't have much to complain about. Especially not after last night and this morning.

"Please put some clothes on before you go outside, Luce!"

Swearing under his breath, Luce reached into his suitcase for something to put on. He found a sock. A single black sock. Well, that wasn't going to cover much and Mel might think it wasn't enough. Sighing, he looked around for something – anything – that wasn't still soaked from its tumble in the washing machine that morning. Well, it qualified as clothing.

He set the wet clothes out in the early morning sun and grabbed the empty basket. The sound of a timid knock on the front door made him set it down again. "Mel, are we expecting visitors?"

"No," she called back. "But we're out of dry towels. I think you used the last one. So hopefully that's Greg with some fresh ones." She paused and Luce heard nothing but the shower before she added, "You are wearing something, right, Luce?"

"Yes. I'll get the door." He threw open the door to find a frightened-looking woman with her arms full of flowers. At her feet was a box of wine and a stack of fresh towels.

"Delivery? For Miss Melody Angel?" the woman stammered.

He'd completely forgotten about the flowers he'd ordered for Mel. "She's in the shower. I'll take it." He held out his arms for the liliums. Luce carried the vase over to the table, where it took up most of the space, before returning for the towels. The woman was already hurrying down the steps. "Thanks," Luce called after her.

She aimed one more frightened look at him and quickened her pace, almost sprinting to her car.

Luce shrugged and hugged the sun-warmed

towels. They easily filled a shelf in the bathroom cupboard. He hung one over the towel rail for Mel and headed back out for the case of wine. He left it on the kitchen bench, figuring he'd ask Mel later where she wanted it.

"Oh, that's so sweet of you to get me flowers, Luce. They smell Heavenly, too."

Luce spun on the spot, startled by her sudden appearance.

Mel wore a skirt and sweater, but the skirt was too long to show her underwear as she leaned over to inhale the flowers' fragrance. She resumed combing her damp hair.

"How'd you know they're from me? You haven't read the card yet." Luce nodded at the little envelope. "I'm not the only one who knows you like these."

"Yes, you are, and you're also the only one who knows I'm here." Mel's smile softened as she read the card. "Not your handwriting, though, so you must have ordered these. Is that what yesterday's phone call was about? I figured you were on the phone to the office."

While he enjoyed her thank you kiss, Luce tried to fit the missing pieces together. No, someone knew — whoever'd bought them in the first place. The person who'd stolen his Melody on Valentine's Day. Who'd…she'd…Luce watched, astounded, as Mel shared the memory of her last Valentine's Day evening.

"You ate pizza, alone at home? You should have called me. I'd have treated you like a queen, Mel. All night." He delved deeper into her memory for the reason why. "You didn't like me? I made you feel uncomfortable? You didn't want me to know where you lived? Oh God, Mel, I'm sorry. You damn near hated me and I…"

"You were a demon, Luce, the same as all the other men who'd sent me flowers that day. And I did regret refusing your invitation, though not because I ate pizza alone. You've changed — something most people wouldn't believe possible. Would the man who bought those orchids for me have been able to heal me as miraculously as you did last night? Or even kiss me properly without burning the both of us with the darkness in his soul?" Her eyes filled with tears. "Or been the first man to ever buy me my favourite flowers, knowing they were my favourite, like you did today?"

He didn't need to say a word – she already knew the answer. But he couldn't resist. "The first? Really?"

Mel beamed. "Yes." She glanced down. "And also the first man I've ever seen wear a sock quite like that. It looks somewhat…strained. Please tell me you didn't answer the door in that."

Luce shifted uncomfortably as he pulled off the sock. It had been getting a bit tight. "All my clothes are drying on the balcony and you said to put some clothes on, so…"

She sighed and snatched up his car keys. "I'll go get your spare things out of the car. That should tide you over until the washing's dry tonight. And please take off my nightdress."

Thirty-three

"Where to?" Luce asked as he slid behind the steering wheel, careful to avoid snagging the precious yellow shirt.

Mel clicked her seatbelt into place. "The bakery in town. I've heard their breakfasts are lovely. And after that…we'll see." She wore her impish smile today – the one that said she had secrets she was dying to share, but not just yet.

Luce knew he hadn't a hope in Hell of getting them out of her until she was ready to divulge them. Not even if he tried reading her…

"No, Luce. My heart and soul are open to you, but not all of my thoughts. I share more with you than anyone else." She laughed. "Maybe even my breakfast, if you're willing to let me taste yours."

They drove in silence until he pulled into the parking lot outside the ramshackle building beneath the sign proclaiming it to be the famed bakery with the "legendary brekkie". Australians would shorten anything, Luce thought as they climbed the timber steps to the veranda. Mel led the way between the crowd of mismatched tables and chairs until they reached a pair of hideous armchairs that were fifty years old if they were a day. She sank into the brown striped one, leaving him the mossy green, and picked up a menu.

Mel offered to go up to the counter to place their order, so Luce stretched his legs out and reclined while he waited. He could see Mel through the window, standing under three chandeliers that spanned the five decades his chair had been around. The whole place looked like a retirement home for elderly furniture – too young to be antiques, but too old to be allowed in any modern home-owner's abode.

Mel returned with a bottle of juice and a number on a metal stand. She set them on the table and surprised Luce by sliding onto his lap instead of her own chair. Throwing her legs over the chair's arm, she pulled Luce in for a long kiss.

"Tell me how many people are here, my love," her soul-voice whispered.

"Three behind the counter and in the kitchen, six inside and outside…seven…no, eleven, plus us." Luce felt the energy signatures of a family of four climb the steps to the veranda.

"And how many plan on going surfing today?"

Luce snorted. "None. With the crazy swell left over from yesterday's storm, anyone who's going to is out there now."

"No. One – the cook's planning on going when he gets off work this afternoon. His thoughts are a litany of prayers that there will still be some waves for him." She paused. "No, no need for regret or guilt. I'm trying to help you extend your existing abilities. It may be that your skills don't lie in soul-reading. Well, outside of our bond, of course. Can you tell me what my most ardent desire is right now?"

Probably not his craving for more sex from the sexy angel on his aching lap, Luce decided, pushing deeper into her soul. Ohhh…

Her most ardent desire was for an answer. If she were to offer him dominion over Heaven, Earth or Hell, or a partnership with her, she feared he might choose power over love. She wanted him to tell her his choice.

"Melody, there is no Heaven without you," he whispered, holding his angel tight. "Earth is empty and Hell can offer me no greater pain than to be parted from you, if I lose you. And I speak from experience."

A smothered giggle got their attention. "Um, your order?" The waitress set out their coffee and breakfast on the table between the armchairs while Mel left Luce's lap for her own chair.

Mel accepted a taste of his mushrooms, but

her fat stack of pancakes was far too much for her to finish. She managed just enough of them for the berry compote to stain her lips a tempting shade of red before she offered the plate to Luce. He grinned, plied his fork and made quick work of the column of cakes. Then he leaned across the table to claim a kiss.

"I love you," Mel's soul-voice sighed.

Luce could still feel the warmth of her love as she moved away from him. Triumph buzzed in his brain. Finally, he could reach her soul without touching her.

Mel's thoughts strayed to her need to return to the bakery counter for a takeaway purchase. She invited him to share her thoughts while she was inside.

He watched her head for the counter, where she waited in line for an interminable ten minutes before collecting a foam box so big he could barely see her behind it. Her thoughts drifted over the items in the box and Luce found himself rising to join her at the counter.

"I hope you put extra chocolate sauce in there. Twice as much as the strawberries need. Because the minute I start licking it off fruit,

I'm going to want to lick it off some warmer, smoother curves and to Hell with the strawberries." Luce's words made both Mel and the girl behind the counter blush a deep shade of strawberry. Luce pressed his lips to Mel's neck. "You're sweeter than anything in that box."

Three pots of chocolate sauce disappeared into the box before the girl replaced the lid. "Enjoy the rest of your honeymoon," she said, giggling.

Luce grabbed the box and pulled Mel outside before she could respond. It wasn't until they were safely in the closed car that he said, "You never cease to surprise me. Up until this morning, I'd have sworn your only response to that would've been to tell me off for making the girl feel uncomfortable and for not controlling my libido."

"What makes you think I still won't?" Mel replied, her thoughts fading into fog.

"Nothing. You're an angel, so you're supposed to help me be good. But you wanted to lick warm chocolate off my body as much as I wanted to slide my tongue across yours. And that isn't something I'd expect of an angel as pure as you." He should have been disappointed in finding that Mel had flaws, but Luce found it excited him beyond belief. Maybe Mel would be willing to…

"I'm not perfect," she said softly. "I have desires – yes, strong desires – just like anyone else. I can control them and, on the rare occasions I do indulge, channel the pleasure from them so that no one is harmed. I'm an angel and I don't let my personal wants get in the way of what's right. Compared to the wellbeing of your soul, my desires don't matter."

Luce leaned over and cupped her cheek so her eyes met his. "They matter to me."

Thirty-four

Curiosity drove him to dip into her thoughts as he drove. She watched the road, too, with a gentle hum of happiness in the background of her thoughts. A gust of wind brought down a shower of leaves and an edge of regret crept in – she didn't want this trip to end. Well, nor did he, but he had to make sure she'd completely recovered. A month hadn't seemed like enough, but he could feel the power pulsing from her soul this morning.

Luce's heart froze. Mel had recovered. He'd

succeeded and that meant their holiday was over. Damn.

"The holiday bit, yes," Mel said softly and it took Luce a moment to realise she'd spoken aloud. "If I no longer need to rest, then I must return to my tasks."

"Can't we take another week? Just the two of us? We have the loft for another fortnight. Surely we're entitled to enjoy our holiday, too," Luce pleaded, hating the weakness in his voice. Just the thought of losing her to whatever political crisis needed her next, as he stayed in HELL without her.

"We don't need to return to the office just yet. I have work to do here, and so do you, my love." Luce stared at her and she smiled as she continued, "It's time I took my duties as your mentor seriously. If you won't accept a more experienced mentor, I hope you'll be willing to forgive me if I do things out of order. It's been a long time since I helped a new angel find their place in Heaven and you are unique. If you wish to leave Hell behind, you can. We just need to work out where your talents lie and which angelic choir you feel you wish to work with."

"Leave Hell? You're serious?" Luce couldn't seem to close his mouth. "Never have to go back? But I'd have to work with angels instead of demons. Even if I'm willing, no angel will want to work with me." From the heights of hope, his heart had plummeted again.

"I love working with you," Mel said warmly. "Patrick and Koyane already accept you and I know you and Patrick make a good team. Not all angels dislike you, Luce."

Luce snorted. "And how many dislike you?"

"There are few who would admit to openly disliking me, but there are some who disagree with me, who prefer not to live and work here under my authority. Ones who would prefer an eternity without me in it. Isn't that dislike, though more passive than the way some feel about you?"

Surprised, Luce didn't know what to say. Everyone loved Mel – demons and angels alike. Who could possibly take offence at anything she did? "Name one."

Mel sighed. "Some are fallen angels and they blame any powerful angel who didn't take their side in the Heavenly Battle. And then there's Hades."

"Him? What's he got against you?"

"Persi. When he abducted Persi, I was the one to bring her back out of the darkness. He'll never forgive me for taking Persi from him." She closed her eyes. "Or for not supporting him in his bid to rule Hell."

"He wanted Hell? Let him have it, Mel. I don't want it. Not any more."

She shook her head. "He demonstrated his poor judgement with Persephone. He's not an angel and he probably never will be. That's why he caretakes the Underworld now, and Hell has a different master. It will be challenging to find a different angel to take your place in Hell, but if I must, then I will."

What? That couldn't be right. "You mean the Lord of Hell doesn't have to be a demon?"

"Of course not. You're not a demon and you're the Lord of Hell."

But not for long, Luce swore. She'd let him leave it forever and find something better to do.

Mel pointed at a road up ahead. "Ooh, turn

left here, please. Follow this road all the way — we're headed for the rocks."

They drove in silence until they reached the end of the road — a car park beside some haphazard piles of granite boulders. The strong, salty breeze hit them the minute they left the confines of the car.

Luce jerked his head at the Jaguar. "Do you want me to grab the box?"

Mel shook her head. "No, I'm still stuffed from breakfast. We can come back for morning tea and lunch after I've walked off some of those pancakes. So nice…but so much!"

His fingers closed around hers. "So, where to first?"

"The boardwalk, I think, and then we should go see some of the rock pools. It should be coming up on low tide soon, so it's the best time to see them." As she tugged on his arm, there was little he could do but follow her swift steps. Excitement radiated off her, as if she was a human child and not an angel older than the granite beneath their feet. "I heard that. You called me old. This rock is older than both of us – and you're no younger than me, Luce."

He conceded the point and followed her along the boardwalk. Their steps thumped dully on the damp beams, carrying them closer to the waves. The waves were on Mel's mind, too, and when they reached the bridge he saw why. "You can't…tell me you're not doing that!" he hissed in her ear.

"I can't lie, Luce."

He watched the waves calming into a gentle swell, rippling the surface with the wind. The amount of power it took to control that volume of water would undo all last night's healing and he'd be lucky to be able to carry her home.

Mel laughed. "I'm only doing what you showed me last night. Come closer, my love, and you'll see how." She pulled his arms around her so that her back rested against his chest. "Close your eyes, my love."

He lowered his lids and reached deeper into her soul. He'd never been so deep inside her before – no, not even during sex. He felt her amusement and the pressure of gentle guidance as he followed her focus to the turbulent waters. She was using the power of the waves themselves, spreading it evenly with a gentle touch of her own energy. "Feel me," she whispered, reaching for an incoming wave. Its energy burst like a bubble, trickling into the water beneath. "The next one's yours."

Luce felt the wave rather than saw it, the course of power raising the ripple into a crest that wanted to crash. He pulled the energy from it, concentrating it like he had the flare last night. Mel had used the power to flatten the crests and raise the troughs, hadn't she? Without waiting for her command, Luce reached for the next wave, too. There was more power in this one, but he knew how to seize it now.

He felt Mel's agitation. "Let it go, Luce."

His attention turned to her – only her – as confusion messed with his focus. Let it go where?

Mel screamed as the wave crashed over the boardwalk railing, sending a wash of water over their feet. When she caught her breath, the next sound was far more intelligible. "Luce!

If you'd wanted to see me in a wet t-shirt, all you had to do was ask."

Luce stared at Mel's soaked shirt and skirt. She'd taken the brunt of the water, shielding him from most of it. He'd taken a faceful of brine and his shoes were full of it, too, but he didn't understand how he'd pulled the wave to them instead of calming it as Mel had.

Mel sighed and showed him her memory, for she'd kept her eyes open. The small wave had dissipated, but the unusually large one behind it had increased as he'd bundled the energy of the little one with the other. Then his focus had shifted to Mel and, as he'd still been controlling the wave, it had come racing toward them, too.

"I'm sorry!" he blurted out, but it didn't seem adequate.

Always an angel, she sounded soothing. "It was bad timing on my part, I think. The king wave was headed here anyway and I distracted you at precisely the wrong moment. Good thing I brought a change of clothes — the waves out here are usually unpredictable, even without you messing with them."

Luce shook his head. "You would have diverted it so it missed us completely. I brought it right to you and I felt it building from the energy I'd pulled from the other waves. I'm not messing with them any more. I'll leave the ocean entirely to you."

Mel kissed his cheek. "You're just naturally talented at stirring things up, my love. I'm sure if I needed a volcano to erupt on cue, no one could hold a candle to you."

He'd probably end up making it erupt prematurely, Luce fumed, stomping after Mel. While the wind was blowing the wrong way to send the ash cloud where it would cause the most trouble, not to mention lava. He'd probably bury whatever Mel wanted him to protect.

"Can you unlock the car, please, my love?"

Luce fumbled for the keys and watched as Mel dived into the boot. Maybe her change of clothes included a shorter skirt. Or even shorts…

She pulled out a bundle. Luce got a glimpse of denim before Mel tucked it into the bag that had held the clothes he was wearing this morning. She kissed his cheek and started walking away.

"Hey! I can help you! Wait!" he called, hurrying to catch up.

Mel laughed. "I'm sure you can, my love, but I don't need help getting dressed. I'll just pop into the toilets and I'll be right out again before the spiders know I was there."

He grabbed her around the waist, pulling her against him. "I could help you in other ways."

"You want to join me in a sandy, cobwebbed, long-drop public toilet in the middle of nowhere? Up against the salt-encrusted walls in a cubicle that smells of dead fish? When we have our lovely apartment with a bed and a spa and everything." Her voice had dropped seductively low, so it was even harder to resist her.

Luce licked his lips. "I'd make it memorable for you, so you don't even notice your surroundings. I promise." He sounded desperate, even to his own ears.

Mel's eyes were filled with pity, for she'd evidently heard his desperation, too. "I know you would. Save it for tonight. You'll have me then, I promise." She paused for a suggestive kiss. "But right now I just want to get out of my wet clothes and into dry ones, before that breeze freezes off anything that you'll miss." She cupped her breasts in his hands and winked. "And I want to see those rock pools before the tide turns. Five minutes, Luce." She ducked out of his arms and into the toilets.

Luce paced around the building for what felt like ages before he felt her arms slip around him. "Four minutes, my love. Let's throw these in the car, grab our morning tea and head out to see some crabs."

Moments later, burdened by a small thermos and a paper-wrapped parcel Mel had insisted he bring, they pounded side by side along the boardwalk to the melody of her breathless laughter. Mel's braid bounced against the back of her yellow sweater and Luce slowed up a little to admire the curve of her arse in her perfectly fitted jeans. Beautiful.

Of course it was a perfect day. Too beautiful to waste in a dingy public toilet. Especially one that smelled of rotten fish.

Thirty-five

"I don't think I've ever eaten so much in one meal in my life, Luce!" Mel exclaimed as soon as they were out of earshot of the restaurant. "I don't think I'll walk it all off even if we do visit my friends at the old homestead tomorrow."

Luce chuckled. "Good thing we're walking back to our little loft, then. A nice little warm up before some real exercise." He glanced at her. "If you're up for that, of course."

Mel tucked her arm through his. "Given

how many times you topped up my wineglass, I'm sure you were trying to get me drunk so I'd sleep with you, Luce."

"I'm counting on sleeping with you. It's the bit before sleep I'm crossing my fingers for," Luce replied. "I even had oysters as an entrée. I'm prepared for you, Mel. Anything you want, all night."

Mel's laughter rang out across the dark vineyard. "You don't need oysters or any other aphrodisiac, Luce. Your sex drive alone was legendary before I came along. But I do recall a promise that tonight was for realising one of your fantasies. Perhaps that's why I agreed to drink all that wine with my dinner instead of pouring it out. You still haven't told me what you'd like, my love."

Luce fingered the handcuffs in his coat pocket. "When we get home. I'll tell you when we're in bed together. Then…then you can tell me if we'll do things my way or yours."

"I promised. I keep my promises, Luce." Mel let out a little shriek as she stumbled and almost fell, but Luce righted her in time. He held her to his side as they walked the last few hundred metres along the gravel drive to their temporary home by the lake.

Together, they stumbled up the stairs and into the warmth of the heated apartment, a welcome contrast to the near-freezing air outside. As Luce hung up their coats, Mel said, "Do you mind if I freshen up a little?"

Luce nodded, wondering at her flush, then figured it was probably a combination of wine and exercise in the cold. That gave him a few minutes to freshen up, too.

Off came his shirt and out came the handcuffs. No, not really cuffs – leather restraints, he decided. He slipped the chain between the vertical rungs on the bedhead, so the wrist cuffs lay on the pillow. He didn't know how long Mel would be, so he'd have to hurry if he wanted to be in position when she came out of the tiny bathroom. If he asked her, she'd never agree, but if he surprised her the way he'd planned, she might just give in…

The door started to open and Luce tensed.

"Bloody Hell."

Thirty-Six

Mel blushed. "I haven't worn anything like this in over a century. It's certainly improved — I didn't know they could be even remotely comfortable." She pressed her hand to the lace on her white corseted breast and glanced down. "I thought the stockings were overkill, but it just didn't feel right to wear a corset without stockings. I drew the line at those g-string things, though. There's nothing comfortable about a stringy thing up your bottom. But these are brand-new, too." Mel touched the cotton knickers at her hip.

"They're all to replace the ones that were torn on your judgement day, outside the gates of Heaven. I thought...I thought you should enjoy them, too."

Luce was speechless. From his initial explosion of swearing, now he couldn't do anything but stare at his Melody Angel in the sexiest white lace lingerie he'd ever seen. And here he was, handcuffed to the bloody bed, and he couldn't touch her unless she came closer. Couldn't even take his pants off, though he'd pitched a pop-up tent in them already. Never in his wildest dreams had he thought she'd wear something like this.

Smiling nervously, Mel perched on the edge of the bed. Still out of reach. He could stroke her with his foot, when he wanted to grab her with both hands. This was the best and worst kind of torture imaginable. And yet...

"So, you said you'd explain your fantasy to me when we were home. It's just us here, so confess, my love. Tell me what you'd like." She crept up the bed so she could look into his eyes, just beyond his grasp. "Or I'll kiss you and you can show me, if it's one of those graphic images Sptlk must have gotten from inside your head."

The imp had a dirty imagination all his own, Luce fumed, swallowing as he tried to form words. He blinked furiously, remembering what the imp had said about illusions being dispelled or returned. He was the lowly angel who didn't deserve her. Blink. He was the Lord of Hell, seducer of thousands, who were all practice for his perfect angel…who he didn't deserve. No, the imp's illusion switch was broken. Ah, to Hell with it.

He jingled the chain linking his wrist restraints. "I'm chained to the bed. Yours. Yours to do…whatever you want with. Without me interfering, or being able to do anything to stop you. You can do anything you want to me."

Mel seemed to be waiting for more. "That's your complete fantasy? I have free reign over your body for…anything? Was there something you wanted me to do? Surely if you've fantasised about this, you have some idea."

Luce shook his head firmly. "No. That

part's up to you. The surprise of not knowing what you'll do and being powerless to stop you…I made this body perfect for you, Mel. Surely you can think of things you'd like to try with it. With me. Hey, you have the Lord of Hell at your mercy. The sleazy devil who made your work life Hell in the office. What's your pleasure, Melody Angel?"

This was a horrible idea, Luce decided as his heart sank. She'd never agree and he may as well throw the cuffs into the lake, for all the use they'd get.

Mel darted in and kissed him, then pulled back before he could reach her. "All right," she began, inspecting his body. "I think the pants should go." She unbuttoned and unzipped, then Luce lifted his hips to help her undress him.

Clad only in his black silk boxers, Luce tensed as he waited to see what she'd do next. She wouldn't hurt him, would she?

Mel tilted her head. "I think…I want you to turn over, so you're lying on your tummy, Luce. Can you do that with those things on your wrists? I can help."

Luce crossed his wrists and struggled to flip his body over without using his arms. It wasn't until Mel's firm hands slid under his back, lifting and turning, that he managed to flop down on the bed, face first.

"These need to go, too, I think." Mel slid her hands into the waistband of his boxers and her warm fingers were softer than any silk, caressing his legs as she stripped him naked. Then she wasn't touching him at all. "I…I need to go get something. I'll be right back." Luce heard her footsteps pad across the tiles away from the bed. Distantly, he heard the squeak of a zip before her bare feet padded back. "There." Something landed on the timber bedside table, but he couldn't see what it was.

What if she was going to hurt him? Hit him with something and then heal him later? What if…

Mel's hand touched his bare arse as the bed shifted to take her weight. Maybe she'd brought sex toys in the hope that he'd be willing to try something kinky. Like he'd refuse. Mel, into kinky sex? This could be fun.

Warm, silky stockings brushed against his hips as Mel perched herself over this thighs. "Okay, this is supposed to help." Something cold and hard touched his back between his shoulder blades. Mel ran it over his back like she was greasing a baking dish. Was she going to set fire to him? This was a mistake. He should never have…

"You're terribly tense, my love." Her lips gently kissed the back of his neck. "Are you sure I'm doing this right?"

"Yes." The word was out before he'd thought it through. She could do whatever she wanted to him. No matter what.

"Relax, my love," she whispered as her hands stroked his back, trailing down to his legs as her weight lifted off him. The bed squeaked as she moved off the mattress entirely, but her warm fingers on his foot reassured him that she wasn't going anywhere. Her thumbs circled against the soles of his feet, her fingers pressing hard enough to probe muscle without tickling him. She finished up by pulling each of his toes between her fingers, stretching each one and releasing the tension in each digit as she did so.

She began tracing elongated figure eights up and down his calf muscles, the firm pressure bordering on painful until he remembered she'd said to relax. And he did, with a blissful groan. Oh God, there was magic in her hands as all the residual stiffness from yesterday's stair climbing vanished as if it had never been. She moved her sensual massage up to his thigh muscles and he was embarrassed to hear himself moan, but Mel didn't seem to notice.

Oh, no, wait, she had noticed and she was trying to hide her amusement. Luce was mortified.

"I said relax, my love. There's no one to hear us and if I'm doing something right, best if you tell me so I can…do a bit more." She sounded breathless and more than a little nervous.

Luce grinned into the pillow and closed his eyes, not caring about anything but her hands on his body. To Hell with being in control any more. He was at Mel's mercy and her ministrations deserved a response. "You're doing everything right. Don't stop, Mel."

She moved to his other leg, soothing away years' worth of tension as he sighed with pleasure. "All right, time to pay some attention somewhere else," she murmured, laying a line of kisses up the back of one leg, then the other. She laughed softly before he felt her soft touch on his right bum-cheek, then the left, leaving a slight coolness behind.

"Did you just…?" He couldn't finish it. She hadn't. She wouldn't…not Mel!

He could hear her smiling. "I just kissed your very sexy arse, Luce. Twice. But now I need to…" The mattress shifted beneath him as she settled her weight on his tingling arse, silk sliding against his hips again as she mounted him.

"Anything," he breathed. "Do anything you wish. Do you want me to turn over?" Please, please let me turn over, he prayed, ready to burst at the thought of being between her silk-clad thighs.

A gentle kiss landed between his shoulder blades, followed by her warm hands. "No, I have you right where I want you for now, my love. A little later, maybe…"

Her hands lightly stroked his shoulders and back, then dug deeper into his shoulder muscles, freeing up what had to be a century of stress.

"Oh my God, Mel," he groaned into the pillow, almost losing all control of his body when she did it again. "Don't stop. Please don't stop. Please…ohhhh, yess…"

She peppered his back with kisses between deep, powerful strokes that left him moaning incoherently. Bliss. This was bliss. Better than sex. And they hadn't even had sex tonight. Oh God, if the sex she had planned was better than the foreplay, he was going to set the sheets on fire the moment she…

"Now turn over, please, my love." She sounded as breathless with desire as he felt.

Eagerly, he grabbed the headboard and flipped from his belly to his back so he could get another eyeful of his beautifully corseted angel. She crept closer, meeting his gaze with a seductive smile as she straddled him. The heat of her thighs on his was going to make him combust. Explode. Burn up like a meteor in the atmosphere.

"Luce, I can't bear it any more. I want…"

"So do I." He pinched a link of chain between his superheated fingertips and it crumbled to ash. Finally free, he sat up swiftly and seized her. His kiss couldn't convey just how much he needed her, but he gave it a damn good try anyway.

She yielded to his fierce kisses for a moment before she burst into laughter. "You mean you could break out of those handcuffs any time you wanted to?"

Luce shrugged. "Of course. Lord of Hell, the hottest devil around…but I'm at your mercy. Whatever you want."

"I missed a spot. I can't bear to see you in pain, Luce."

Yes! Those cotton knickers would come off and she'd finally…

Mel's gentle fingers unbuckled one of the restraints. Her thumb circled his palm, relaxing his hand like nothing else. She stroked his fingers, pulling gently and releasing tension he didn't even know he had. She turned her ministrations to his other hand, then kissed his wrists. "You don't need to go through that for me. Ever. Just seeing you restrained made me ache in sympathy, Luce. I hope they weren't too tight."

Luce laughed and picked up one of the discarded restraints. "Soft, white leather...padded and lined. The only kind of cuffs an angel would use on someone she cared for. You did miss a spot, my sweet angel, where there's far more tension straining to be released than I've ever had in my hands." He glanced down and Mel's gaze followed.

Her hands gently stroked, increasing the tension to heights he hadn't believed possible. He groaned, unable to stop himself.

"It's all right, my love. I'll take care of you. I was keeping the best for last." She kissed him lightly.

Luce closed his eyes in bliss as Melody flew him to Heaven.

Thirty-Seven

Mel let her body relax into sleep and carefully disengaged from her exhausted flesh. Her soul felt fresher than ever, but she lingered to look. Luce lay beside her, cradling her in his arms as if she was the most precious thing he had on this Earth. The love in his expression as he looked at her sleeping form…such tenderness. She couldn't fathom how anyone could believe he was still a demon, incapable of redemption or love.

She hovered just above his face and allowed

the slightest illumination to show her soul's form. It had been a long time since she'd done such a thing, and she'd forgotten the tingle her soul experienced from it. Like sitting in a bath of freshly poured champagne. She laughed.

"Are you just going to stare at my sleeping body all night, or are you coming out to play?" she asked.

Luce's arms tightened around her back as he touched his lips to her hair. Mel felt the overpowering urge to return to her body to feel his caresses. No, her corporeal form needed rest. Let her soul fly until morning.

"It's tempting. I could watch you sleep forever. I don't want to take my eyes off you for fear you'll disappear like a dream I know I don't deserve." Luce lifted his eyes to her faintly glowing soul.

"Then dream with me, my love." She reached for him.

"Where are you going? I'll only be a burden if you're working. Unless you plan another trip around the sun."

Her light brightened in its expression of the smile she couldn't show. "The sun has seen enough of me this century. We're not supposed to take too much of its power, or we'll shorten a star's lifespan. The power can be addictive, too, to those not accustomed to showing restraint." Like you, my love, she thought but didn't say. He seemed to understand this without her assistance. "Tonight, I plan on staying close to my body. I wish to watch the stars from this side of the planet's atmosphere and perhaps see some of the nocturnal creatures who call this place home. I understand if you wish to do something other than share owls and stars with me, my love."

"After an evening like you gave me tonight, I'll do anything for you. No matter how strange it sounds. Yours, forever and always, Melody." He kissed her hair one more time and closed his eyes. Almost instantly, his soul rose from his sleeping body. "There. That was easier than I thought. Now it's my turn to lift you to Heaven." His soul enveloped hers and she laughed at the warmth of him as he buoyed her up, through the roof and into darkness.

"So I didn't do too badly, then?" Mel asked shyly. "I've never been someone's fantasy before, Luce. This was definitely a first for me. I hope I didn't miss doing anything important. You never did tell me what you wanted." She'd deliberately waited until he was out of his body and unable to conceal anything from her before she asked. She knew she'd surprised him, but she still felt uneasy about the whole experience.

Luce's laughter was a deep vibration. "Melody, you incinerated all my fantasies the moment you appeared in that white corset, you looked so hot. I was afraid to ask for anything else – anything I thought of just paled in comparison. So I surrendered to your angelic charms and my soul is still singing for joy. Listen." Faintly, she heard Beethoven's Ninth Symphony drifting on the night breeze and it was her turn to laugh.

"You've been through my music collection," she admonished.

"You should have been there for its first performance in Vienna. I've heard better renditions since, with better acoustics and far more practice before the performance, but…"

Mel stared at him. "My love, I was. I never saw you in the Kärntnertortheater. But I was very much taken with the music and I wasn't working. I'm sure you wouldn't have noticed me in the crowd, even if you did see me."

"I only wish I had," Luce said, echoing her own thought. He broke the mood with a surge of hot lust. "And if I'd known you were capable of half of what you did tonight, I'd have fallen to my knees and begged the moment I met you."

"My sexy devil," Mel murmured. "Can we sit still and watch the stars for a few hours without you thinking of sex?"

"Hell no," he responded. "Not when I know you're not wearing anything. And after what you did earlier with your…"

"Shh, Luce."

Thirty-eight

Luce squinted into the windows, shading his eyes with his hand against the bright morning sun. "I can't see any furniture and it doesn't look like anyone's here. Who have we come to see again?"

Mel laughed and pulled Luce away from the old wattle and daub house. "That's because they never lived in the house. This belonged to some early European settlers. My friends lived in a cave to the south and I'll show you." She lowered her gaze and her voice. "This is…a very personal place for me. I've never brought anyone here before and it's been a very long time since I've seen it. Even the local people never came here. They told stories of a devil bird who lived in this place, which frightened away all but the most curious."

"How anyone could mistake you for a devil, I don't know," Luce said with a grin.

Mel didn't return it. "To the dark-skinned people who lived here, devils were pale. And this one was the size of a human with huge, white wings. Please, Luce, you showed me your personal place in Hell – Hell's bathroom, the beautiful cave you shared with me. I'd like to show you what the locals here once called the bathing place of the moon, Meekadarrabee."

Something in her tone caught him and his soul reached for hers. There was sadness and loss in this place for Mel, yet she longed to share it with him. Luce took her hand and her thoughts sharpened as her bubble of worry burst with relief. She feared this place held too much pain for her to visit alone and she wanted to ask for his support. But if he treated it like a joke, her pain was too raw to allow him any closer to the place and she would keep her secrets to herself. "I'd be honoured," he found himself saying.

Mel's smile was shy as she led him up the hill and into the bush.

The sweet smell of peppermint was stronger here – like that rock candy shop near the office, Luce mused. The bushes to either side of the track were dotted with butterfly-shaped flowers in purple and orange and pink. And the occasional orange butterfly, he realised as what he'd thought was an unusual patterned flower took flight.

He caught glimpses of the swift-flowing creek between the trees – the same Ellen Brook that flowed beside the house on its way to the sea.

"The path never used to be this clear," Mel murmured as her grip tightened around his fingers. "The easiest approach was to find the mouth of the stream and fly up the watercourse to the spring at its source. Of course, I could only do this at night, which earned me the name of Nyoorlam among the local people who saw me. Nyoorlam means devil bird or night hawk."

"One night, I'd love to fly beside you," Luce replied.

Mel just smiled and drew him on. She didn't stop until they reached a clearing that ended in a wall of rock with a small pool at its base. Luce could hear water trickling and he leaned over to see that the wall wasn't as solid as it seemed – it was the entrance to a cave, and the exit for the stream that fed the pool.

Mel swallowed a few times before she said, "One night, I went for a swim in the pool and I didn't realise there were curious eyes watching me. When I emerged from the water, shaking the droplets off my skin, a girl's voice told me that I didn't look as scary as a demon. More like the moon, shimmering on the surface after her bath." Her smile reappeared, but it looked watery. "I remember I laughed and told her that I wouldn't harm her, so in that, I was more like the moon than a demon. That was the extent of her courage that night. She returned to her people, who were camped nearby at a place called Mokidup.

"The following night, she returned. She was stealthy, but I was expecting her. She sat on the bank of the stream and announced that she'd told her grandmother about me. Her grandmother was an elder, and her response was to tell the girl she was cursed for daring to find the bathing place of the moon. I said I didn't know of any curse and she was welcome to join me if she wished, but she didn't.

"Instead, she just sat on the bank of the stream, swinging her legs as I listened to the stories that spilled from her lips. She told me of caves and forests and secret places she'd found as she explored. And then…she rose and ran off."

A gust of wind caught the branches above, sending down a cascade of tiny white flower petals and a whiff of peppermint. Mel laughed, lifting her face to the sky.

Luce's mouth went dry. His precious angel, haloed in sunlight as the petals drifted down like snow. Heaven. He was in Heaven just watching her.

Mel's fingers slid between his. "Come on. I want to show you the waterfall before I tell you the rest of the story." Dazed, he followed her, as he knew he always would.

They stopped abruptly at an official sign that informed them that the track was closed due to severe erosion. Luce couldn't help laughing — the danger sign and caution tape were wrapped around the framework of a bridge across a muddy creek. The severe erosion had carried away the whole damn bridge and the new one was nowhere near finished yet.

He shrugged. "I've learned my lesson. Last time I ignored one of these signs I ended up on my arse in a cold creek. Guess we'd better head back." He turned to lead the way.

Mel's fingers tightened around his. "No. I've never needed a bridge to reach the falls and there is a bridge — look." She pointed at some mud-encrusted planks laid across the shallow creek. "We'll be fine." When Luce didn't move, she tugged on his arm. "Trust me, Luce. I'll even go first."

Of course he trusted her. But where she'd cross the creek as clean as if she'd taken the non-existent bridge, he'd probably slip and end up starting a legend of a mud monster here.

Mel winked. "I'll break out my wings and carry you across if you're scared, Luce."

His eyes on the mud, Luce felt a grin spreading across his face. "I trust you, but if I do end up in the creek, I want your promise that this afternoon we'll be mud wrestling." Just the thought of their bodies twined together, slipping and sliding in the slick mud, was worth whatever trouble he got into beforehand.

Mel laughed, a musical sound that was picked up by hidden birds overhead. "Sure, my love. But I get to be on top." She trotted gracefully down the bank and across the first plank, then the second. Her fingers curled around a sapling before Mel sprang up the opposite bank, resting her hand on one of the bridge supports. Balancing carefully on the other end of the bridge frame, she called, "C'mon, Luce. The falls aren't much further."

His eyes firmly fixed on his angel, Luce stumbled and slid down the slope. The first plank sent up small splatters of mud with every heavy footfall, but it didn't throw him into the water. The second plank was laid across only slightly damp soil, so Luce figured he was in the clear when he realised there was a third plank. This was barely visible above the mud and sank deeper with each step, but he made it across that one, too, with only slightly muddied shoes. Hidden by vegetation, the steep slope on the other side had seemed deceptively easy for Mel's ascent, but Luce found it the most challenging bit. Mel's sapling threatened to bend right over beneath his grip and he barely managed to grasp the next one before he slid back down into the creek.

Strong fingers caught his flailing hand and his feet finally found purchase on the slope. He reached the level patch of mud beside the bridge frame where Mel was precariously balanced on a beam before he dared to breathe again. With his first exhalation, he thanked her.

"You know I'll lift you when you fall, my love. Every time." She hopped from beam to beam until she landed on the path again, as agile as the bird the native people had named her.

Luce placed his bigger feet carefully on the

beams, making sure each would take his weight before he moved to the next one. He felt unusually proud of himself when he reached Mel's side on the overgrown track.

She grabbed his hand, the energy of her eagerness fizzing through the contact, and it was all he could do to keep up with her as she led the way through the pile of lumber that presumably waited to complete the bridge and the mess of clinging branches that tried to squeeze the track out of existence. Pushing aside one more armload of whippy branches, they stepped into the final clearing where the falls cascaded down the mossy stones.

Mel led Luce to a bench beside the falls and sat, waiting for him to squeeze in beside her before she said, "And now the part I've never told a soul."

Thirty-nine

"A few years later, I returned, winging my way from the sea, wanting nothing more than peace after the conflicts I'd seen elsewhere. The moment I descended below the canopy, I knew I was being watched, but I had no need to hide my wings then as I do now. The water was cool from its time in the cave and so refreshing that it was all I could think about, yet the watching eyes hadn't left. I rose from the pool and faced the girl I'd seen on my previous visit, though now she'd grown into a woman. And she wasn't alone. A young man stalked the shadows behind her.

"I wondered whether to warn her, but she beat me to it, beckoning the boy to the bank by her side. She told me her name was Mitanne and Nobel was her beloved. They lived here at Meekadarabee – the bathing place of the moon – because their tribes wouldn't allow them to be together. He usually hunted at night, but the devil bird flying through the skies tonight had frightened everything into hiding. He'd need to travel further afield if they were to eat tomorrow, he said, before he kissed her goodbye and headed off into the bush. It was…sweet to see them together. How tenderly he touched her for just a moment, yet that moment held so much love…" Mel closed her eyes and sighed. A tear slid down her cheek. "I'm telling this wrong. Please…let me show you the memory?"

Luce nodded and she cuddled up to him, taking his hands in hers. His eyes snapped shut as he reached for her soul and was surprised at the clarity of Mel's memory.

He watched the scrub fly past as if he was

running through it, following a track through the underbrush that only he knew. A game trail, perhaps. The sun sank and the stars started to prick the darkening sky. Wings above obscured the stars for a moment before they were gone, silent flight carrying the creature away, but still she followed it, increasing her speed. A flash of white ahead made her slow her pace before she sank to her knees on the edge of the clearing. Before her, glowing faintly in the starlight, a pale female form stood waist-deep in the water. Her wings faded from sight and she sighed, stretching out to float on her back on the rippled surface.

Luce recognised Mel in the water and confusion jolted him halfway out of the memory. If the memory was Mel's, then why was she seeing herself?

"The memory is Mitanne's, as she shared it with me. You see?" Mel murmured.

Luce watched his perfect angel bathing in the distant past and became aware of the dark-skinned hands pushing the bushes aside as Mitanne emerged from her hiding place. Her heart had swelled just as Luce's did at Mel's sweet smile. Luce longed to join her in the water, but the girl remained resolute on the bank. She believed Mel to be the moon herself, come to Earth to grace this place with her light, and the girl wasn't worthy to share such a sacred place.

The girl spoke in words Luce didn't understand, but the images in her mind were clear. As she described places to Mel, she recalled the plants and animals, rocks and watercourses she'd encountered. The beady black eye of a striped numbat, the musical cry of a hundred black cockatoos as they sailed overhead, the quiet drip of water in a cave beside bones too big to belong to any creature she'd ever seen, tingle trees so huge their trunks were large enough for a whole tribe to shelter inside, the sweet smell of peppermint bushes here and the flash of ocean-blue in the trees as a tiny bird with bright blue feathers darted between branches. And the echo of Mel's remembered laughter in the clearing as she said she brought no curse.

Luce felt a shiver as the girl's deeply held beliefs whispered that she was cursed, no matter what the friendly devil bird said, edged by Mel's sorrow at the memory.

The scene changed. The bushes were thicker and higher, and the girl's fingers were longer as she pushed the leaves aside to reach Mel's pool. She brushed a fly off her perspiration-beaded breast, longing to feel the coolness of the cave water on her skin. The water only came to her thighs, for without winter rainfall to swell the pool, it was much shallower in the baking heat of summer, but she plunged in again and again, sharing the moon's love for her private bathing place.

Her skin prickled as she felt eyes on her and she rose from the water, scanning the vegetation until she met the gaze of her unseen watcher. He rose from the bushes, placing his spear butt-first against the stone beside him. "Are you the devil bird who bathes in this pool?" he demanded, showing no fear.

She admired his courage, but she laughed and asked him what he would do if she was.

He stood straighter and replied, "I would impale you on my spear and carry your body as a trophy to my people. Then all would only speak of me in whispers, of how powerful a hunter Nobel must be, to have conquered the demon."

Her memory sparked with faint images of a boy her own age from another tribe, who she'd occasionally seen when their tribes were both in the same region. He had been something like a playmate then, but nothing like the strong man he had become. Perhaps this fearless hunter could carry her away from the curse her grandmother had placed on her – her betrothal to a tribal elder, a great honour she didn't want. She shivered whenever the elder looked at her, his eyes filled with a fire of longing that frightened her.

She told him her name and her tribe – names that were meaningless to Luce – before he felt a stirring of lust that was both familiar and alien. The girl's reckless desire drove her to cast caution to the wind and she invited Nobel to join her in the pool. He impaled her, all right, but he left his wooden weapon on the bank as the two made love in the water. She begged him to sneak into her camp under the cover of darkness and steal her away.

Some nights later, after her people had moved on and set up camp much further away, she was woken by a hand over her mouth to silence her. It took her a moment to recognise the young man from the pool and quell her fear enough to creep out of the camp and away with him. They ran all night and into the next day before they reached Mokidup. Instead of living in the camping place alone, they slept in the cave, hunting the rich lands here and bathing together in the pool to slake their desire. Their combined laughter echoed off the rocks, banishing the curse that lay over her, or so the girl thought.

And then the moon maiden appeared again, the pale devil bird who had given Mitanne permission to visit this place. Luce tasted the girl's cocktail of emotions – fear, bravado, protectiveness and desire for the boy, who'd hidden from the strange winged woman. Mitanne had told Nobel about the true devil of the pool and she didn't want him to be cursed for offending her. So she lied about there being no game here and how he needed to hunt away from here that night, her eyes begging him to understand. Relief flooded through her when he nodded and set off across the ridge to hunt.

Luce's phone trilled, jerking him halfway back to reality. He shoved his hand in his pocket and jabbed at the power button, holding it down until the trilling faded to silence. To Hell with the outside world of the present – he was busy with Mel.

Mel's memory seemed edged by sadness now, he realised as he focussed on the long-ago night time scene. Uneasily, he wondered whether the girl or the boy was going to fall victim to the imaginary curse.

The scene blurred until the sky was streaked with pink from the approaching dawn. Distant shouts carried on the wind. Mitanne's panic sent her sprinting toward the sound, along the trail Nobel had taken east to hunt in the lee of the ridge, leaving the devil bird far behind. She heard them before they noticed her – a band of hunters from her tribe, clustered around Nobel, accusing him of crimes against her tribe for which the punishment was death. Crossing into lands and hunting grounds that were forbidden. Theft of the elder's bride, kidnapping her and keeping her from her rightful husband and tribe. Trespassing on the sacred ground at the waterfall. He shook his head and denied all of it. He was on permitted land now, hunting as he'd been ordered, not land that was forbidden or sacred. And where was this bride he'd supposedly carried off? Did they have her?

Mitanne heard it all and faded into the bush, barely daring to breathe in fear that they might discover her hiding place, for the elder had sent her tribe's best hunters in pursuit of her.

She watched in horror as one of the men picked up Nobel's own spear and thrust it through the boy's body, pinning him to the sand. His agony was written clearly across his face, but Nobel didn't make a sound, such was his courage. The hunters pointed toward the sea and the cave where she and Nobel had made their home, then set out along the trail for the coast.

Mitanne waited until she could no longer hear them before she rushed to Nobel's side. She was no medicine woman and the sand was sticky with his blood, he'd lost so much, but she held him and spoke words of love to him as her tears washed the blood from his face. He said little, for he only had moments left to live as his lifeblood drained from his body, but he told her he loved her before he died in her arms.

Luce felt tears on his own face at the memory of losing Mel in much the same way outside Heaven's gates. The wave of despair that engulfed the girl as her beloved breathed his last washed over Luce as surely as the human girl. He felt Mel's arms tighten around him now, though, as her love softened the sharp pain of the girl's memories.

The girl didn't know how long she stayed with Nobel's body, calling down curses on her people for killing the man she loved, and on herself for causing him to be cursed by the moon. Her memories were blurred as rough hands seized her and carried her through the bush, though she saw none of it in her haze of grief. She found herself back in her tribe's camp, numbly obeying the orders of anyone who had work that needed to be done. This was her punishment for deserting her tribe — she would be made to do all the hardest work until she had earned the honour of being the elder's bride. She ceased eating and drinking, wishing only to return to the pool where she and Nobel had laughed and loved for such a short time.

One day, while carrying a heavy load of wood for the fire, she stumbled and fell. Such was her weakness that she couldn't seem to get up, so she accepted assistance when it was offered. When she rose, she came face to face with Nobel and a man she didn't know. The hand had belonged to the devil bird, who now stood beside her.

The memory faded into fog there, but Luce couldn't get that last image of Mel out of his head. The weeping angel who stood beside the girl.

"What happened to her?" he asked thickly, finding that she wept just as freely now, a waterfall that flowed down her cheeks like the cascade on the other side of the clearing.

"She died. Exhaustion and thirst and a broken heart. She didn't want to live any more and the angel who took Nobel's soul knew she wouldn't be far behind him, so he waited to collect them both before taking them to wherever they were destined to go."

Just as he'd tried to, Luce thought, in the depths of Hell and despair without Melody. Only he hadn't lingered. He'd taken a weapon to his veins to hasten the end. Pity devils couldn't die. But if they could, he wouldn't be holding his sweet, weeping angel in his arms, as she cried her heart out for a human. The human couple's doomed love would never be their fate – he'd never desert Mel, nor lose a fight to a bunch of humans armed with nothing but spears. They'd stand side by side against anyone who dared to threaten them. He pulled his handkerchief out of his pocket and pressed it to her cheek. "And you've never shown this to anyone." When Mel shook her head, he added, "Why did you share it with me?"

Mel took the handkerchief from his hand and it faded from black to gold with shocking speed before it even reached her other cheek. "Because I knew you would understand her pain. The pain of a human, my love, which was just as poignant as yours. I've seen billions of people die – through violence and illness and age – but her life and death were the first to touch me so personally, because I felt it all as I lifted her soul from her body. You asked once why angels would allow humans into Heaven, when there were so many who did not belong there, and none of the angels in Heaven could answer you, though they took up arms against you. She had your answer, my love. The souls of her kind feel as acutely as any of us – with pain and joy and love. Maybe not all human souls belong in Heaven, but there are demons among our kind who have no place there, either. And some even get to be angels – like Patrick."

Luce wet his lips. "If I'd asked you instead of those stuck-up angels in Heaven, would you have answered me? Prevented the Heavenly War and all the pain afterwards?" Oh God, if she could have saved him from millennia of darkness…

"Would you have listened?"

No. He didn't even need to consider it. He,

the highest of them all, listen to the reasoning of a lowly Domination about the flawed beings he despised? His pride would have made him laugh in her face. Pride would have been his downfall, all the same.

"Don't be so hard on yourself, my love. The memory was still too raw for me to discuss with even those closest to me, let alone some mighty angel I barely knew. I might not have said a word to you about it then. Even now, I can't look at the pool without hearing their laughter in the water's play, though they are both long gone. And if I hadn't been here, if she hadn't seen me…if Mitanne had chosen to accept the fate her grandmother arranged for her, she'd have been the elder's adored wife and one of the most respected women elders among her people. She could have been a leader who —"

He felt her grief like a punch in the gut. "No. Don't you blame yourself for what happened to them. They're human and humans have free will to make their own choices and their own mistakes. They knew the justice system of their people and the consequences of their actions. That your kind heart still feels sorry for them is an honour for their memory and a compliment to your compassion. If their love hadn't touched you, would you have become the sweet angel who saved me, or just another stuck-up statue, incapable of feeling love or pity for something as damaged as me?"

"You're not damaged." Mel seized him, crushing her mouth against his as her soul overflowed with gratitude for his help in allowing her to put the spirits of her past to rest.

On and on he kissed her, dimly aware of the petals floating down like snow as the waterfall giggled to itself in the background. It wasn't until the gurgling in his stomach drowned out the watery sounds that Mel broke contact to laugh. "I'm sorry, my love. We should go get the picnic basket out of the car and have some lunch. I know a lovely, secluded spot down by the old waterwheel." Her fingers laced securely through his, they walked hand in hand back to the car.

Forty

He kicked the door shut behind him before
Mel pinned him to the wall, kissing him
fiercely as she helped him unbutton his shirt.
He knew they should've thrown caution to the
wind and made love on the grass instead of
waiting until they got home. She was as eager
as he was, but she was also insistent that she
wanted privacy. This from the angel who'd
walked through Hell naked. What did it matter
if someone saw them?

Oh, damn it, not again!

Luce pried his lips from Mel's to answer his persistent phone. "Yes?"

"Mr Iblis, I'm so sorry to bother you, but she wouldn't take no for an answer. Bob tried to throw her out, but she banished him back to Hell. Level Eight for a year! Just for following your orders. I can feel his pain even here! And she said she'll do the same to me if I don't call you. I didn't think she could DO that…did you put her in charge of Hell and not tell me?" Mephi had never sounded so upset. Hell, it sounded like there were tears.

Luce ground his teeth. "You tell Lili to go back to Hell and leave the company to Beelzebub. She doesn't have the authority to tell either of you what to do — all she's responsible for is Level Seven in Hell. You've never had any trouble putting her in her place before. Pull rank, Mephi."

A high-pitched sob came through the phone. "It's not Lili, Mr Iblis. I don't know what to do. I tried to order her out of your office — well, Bob's office, but she just laughed. She had Bob on his knees under the desk, his face buried deep in her tattoo of Level

Eight...my husband! She turned my husband into a gigolo in front of my eyes and wouldn't let him stop until she was satisfied, then sent him to Hell before she closed her skinny legs. She said if you don't appear before her in HER office today with Miss Angel, it'll be me next!"

On her knees or in Level Eight? Luce wondered idly, before his fingers clenched around the phone. "Persephone. That bitch. She's had Mel and I combing the world for her, and she turns up in the office now? Oh, I'll be there, all right. We both will. And I'm going to peel that tattoo off her body with a bloody box cutter." Luce glanced at his watch. "We're four hours away. Tell her we'll meet her in MY office at six. And Mephi?"

"Yes, Mr Iblis?"

"Make dinner reservations for Mel and I for seven. Pick the best restaurant within walking distance of the office. If I have to cut our holiday short, I need to make it up to her."

"Yes, Mr Iblis."

Mel leaned in close so her cheek was right beside Luce's. "Mephi? It's Mel. Once you've done what Luce asked, go home. Take the rest of the day off and go find your husband. When you're together again, you go out for a fancy dinner, too. Maybe Japanese. Teppanyaki, if you think Bob's up for that."

"Miss Angel? Are you all right? Miss Black kept asking about you. Your health, your happiness…everything. When I told her you appeared tired, she killed my pot plant. One minute it was a small army of yellow-bordered green spikes, the next it crumbled into dust."

Luce felt Mel's consternation. "Do what Mel said, Mephi. And…one last thing. Book a cleaning crew for first thing tomorrow. A demon one, not a human one. This won't end without bloodshed." Luce ended the call.

Mel didn't need telling. She swept around the room, collecting her things and piling them neatly in her suitcase. Fifteen minutes later, she started on Luce's suitcase, worry creasing her forehead into premature wrinkles he wished he could ease away.

"I'm sorry, Mel," Luce said. "I wanted to give you a proper holiday, not pull you into the problems of the HELL Corporation. Now my former PA has come back to bite me. I swear to you I'll make this right."

"I know you will. No holiday can last forever, my love. Thank you for the best I've ever had. It's been wonderful." Mel's kiss was soft, but tinged with sadness. "Whether she comes at my summons or issues her own, I must meet with her. She wanted to become an angel. For her actions, she must face judgement."

Luce snorted. "Sounds to me like she wants Hell, not Heaven, after what she did."

The zip buzzed closed before Mel set his suitcase on the floor beside hers. "There. Can you load these and the wine in the car while I pack the remainder of our food into a box? If we get going in the next hour, we'll have time for a shower before our meeting and dinner."

"Together, I hope," Luce replied as he hefted the suitcases.

"That sounds lovely," he heard Mel say as he headed down the stairs.

Forty-one

Her office looked untouched since she'd left for London, Mel mused as she glanced around the immaculate space. The only exception was her in tray on the desk — in the last month, it had grown a neat stack of papers. Idly, she picked up the first one and checked the cover page. Mel couldn't smother her laughter when she realised it was a report on monumental cane toad dumping, courtesy of her new complaints department. She wondered at the big Q logo on it — evidently some new form of corporate branding she'd investigate in the morning.

Luce's happy sigh as he entered the room made her smile, but the burst of love she felt emanating for him was far more eloquent. Mel closed her eyes as his arms pulled her against his chest.

"I can't keep my hands off you when you wear the gold silk dress. I've dreamed about this. I don't know if I want to bend you over the desk and slide that skirt up over your hips or drop to my knees and worship you, Lady Muriel." Luce's voice was husky with lust and she could feel his every muscle hard against her back. Oh yes, definitely every muscle.

"Where are your clothes?" she murmured.

His lips caressed her neck. "Hanging up in my office. I can hang your dress beside them and to Hell with this meeting, if you like." He slid his hand up her thigh, hitching her skirt up to her hip. "If we hadn't gotten stuck in traffic, we'd have had that heavenly shower together. Oh God, Melody, you don't know how much I want you."

She did. She could feel his desire, but also

what lurked beneath it. Carefully, she smoothed her skirt. "Whatever happens tonight, remember that I love you. You have nothing to fear from this meeting, Luce. As long as I'm by your side, she can't hurt you." She pressed her lips together before she said any more. She'd slept in the car and taken a moment to walk the paths of the future – or she had until Luce's swearing at the crawling traffic had woken her. It was enough. She knew what was coming and she didn't want to frighten him further.

"I'm not…" he began, but they both knew he couldn't finish his sentence. He was afraid. If not of Persi, then something else.

Mel stretched up to kiss him, pressing her hands against his hard, red chest to maintain her balance. "My big, sexy devil. If you want to attend this meeting as the powerful Lord of Hell, that's up to you, but THAT will definitely draw attention." She stared pointedly at his groin.

Luce grinned, but his mirth didn't reach his worried eyes. "Maybe that's where I want her thoughts to be. On what's yours and will never be hers." He pulled Mel close again, holding her just that bit tighter to still the shaking she could feel in his hands. "We have twenty minutes before the meeting. Plenty of time for us to christen this desk of yours and release some tension. What do you say?"

Mel sighed. Of course she'd love to give in to her desires and his, but time was ticking away. If only…

"That's it. Get your damn hands off her! That's one angel you can't have."

Too late.

Forty-two

"Go home. This is a private party for the two of us and no one else was invited. Get out of this office!" Luce roared.

No one moved. What the Hell? Demons had always followed his orders before. What was happening?

"I said let her go. She's not yours and you have no right to enslave her like this. Mel's an angel and she should stay that way." Merih's words were drowned out by a raucous rumble of approval.

"There are a lot of demons out there, Luce," Mel murmured, taking a step toward the door. "I think I need to speak to them."

He grabbed her arm. "NO! I can't control them any more. I don't know what they'll do to you and I might not be able to stop them. Mel, it's too dangerous. Let me try to calm them down first…"

"Send her out or we'll drag you out!" Nybbas shouted reedily.

Mel kissed Luce's fingers before she pried them loose. "Calming people down is what I do best. They can't hurt me, Luce." She approached the doorway and Merih stepped aside to let her pass. Luce's heart plummeted as Mel waved her hand as if in farewell as she left.

"No, Mel, I won't let you –" He hit an energy barrier that she'd waved into place behind her. "Damn it, Mel, do you expect me to just stand here and watch while you…you…"

"Walk away. We'll stop him from following you," Merih said grimly, folding his arms. The crowd parted to allow Mel's passage, but closed up behind her so Luce couldn't see her any more. "Head for Heaven, Mel. He can't find you there."

In desperation, Luce shouted, "Go where you'll be safe, Mel. I'll find you. I swear I'll find you."

"No you fucking won't," Geryon said, planting himself beside Merih. "You're going to let her go, even if it takes all of us to rip you apart so you can't pursue her. You can have any human on Earth, but Mel's off limits."

"Let her make her own choices. Ask her!" Luce insisted.

Nybbas stepped up to the barrier. "She's too brainwashed to make the right decision. I don't know what you've done to her, but it's going to stop, right here and right now. We'll get her to Heaven, where they can help her. The other angels will help us keep her away from you!" He reached toward Luce, but the shield emitted a shower of sparks, stopping his hand. "What's this? Some trick to keep us from reaching you? Are you such a coward you need a shield to protect yourself from us? Is this how you kept her prisoner?"

"I can't…it's not my…" Luce pressed his hands against the barrier, shoving with all his strength, but he couldn't push through. Mel's shield was too strong. Yet he could feel her as a calm presence on the other side. If only he could see her and do something to help.

Mel leaped lightly onto the coffee table. Her wings shimmered into being, so big they brushed the ceiling. "The shield is mine. I won't let you hurt him." Her normally clear voice shook.

"We'll carry you to Heaven's gates if we have to." Nybbas swallowed. "Get angels to help us keep him away from you."

They would. Oh Hell, they would – Luce knew every angel in Heaven would do anything they could to keep her away from him. His precious angel, standing on her coffee table pedestal, her inner glow shining through silk and skin. He greedily drank in the sight, wanting to see these mutinous demons burn like the malicious dark souls she'd vanquished in the depths of Hell. Demons who deserved their fate for daring to…try to take her from him. How could his demons possibly resist his authority to the point where they'd disobey his express orders? No demon had ever been able to withstand him before…

Mel surveyed the sea of expectant eyes turned toward her and Luce felt her rising tide of panic. Her throat constricted and her knees weakened. Oh God, what a time for her fear to materialise. She couldn't say a word.

"Leave her alone. Look at her, she's terrified. Mel's not used to violence. Step aside and let her pass and I might let you keep your limbs. NOW!" Luce ordered.

"Shut up!" Merih roared. He pointed at several demons. "Get through that shield and tear him apart if you have to, to stop him following her. The rest of you – help me take her to the gates."

What looked like a hundred hands extended toward Mel as the demons crowded close around her. Luce couldn't see her through the demons sparking at the shield, but he could feel her pain as each touch burned her. "Get out of here and go to Heaven." Luce didn't speak the words aloud – he shouted them from the depths of his soul.

Her soul-voice sounded sweeter than her human one. "I won't leave without you. Won't let them hurt you."

"Then they must burn." He focussed on the image of her soul filling the cave with light outside his Hellish lair. She had to do it again.

"No," she said silently. "They're my colleagues. I can't. I can't hurt them." A flash of pain was followed by her tormented cry and the sound of a body smacking against the wall. Luce glimpsed her face for a moment before another demon came between them. This one was blasted backwards and Luce heard the crack of bone when it hit the wall.

"You can't help hurting them. Every time they touch you, you'll both burn. Get out and head for Heaven. I'll be fine!" He wanted to shout the words, but sent the thought arrowing across the crowd that separated them.

"No, Luce, I love you and won't leave you. I will protect you – even from pain." Her soul-voice ended abruptly as if she'd closed the door and sealed him out. Another impenetrable energy shield. Or had she lost consciousness?

Luce stretched and craned his neck to see above the crowd, but she'd vanished.

She cried out in pain again and Luce's knuckles went white as he gripped the door frame. She was conscious and hurting and he couldn't sense her. To Hell with that.

He closed his eyes and reached for the heated mob. Time to cool things off a little… Luce ripped the heat from air and demonic bodies alike, channelling it into the wall beside the door. Frost formed on the ceiling, but still Luce pulled energy from the room. Mel's energy shield only blocked the doorway, not the whole room, and under his concentrated onslaught the wall crumbled to dust. He strode through the cloud that had once been a wall.

"Don't touch her. Step away from the angel. I won't ask again." Luce put all his fury into his tone and watched in satisfaction as a few edged away from him.

"Speak for yourself. You won't touch her again. She's going to Heaven." Luce couldn't see through the dust cloud to identify the speaker. It didn't matter — their ranks closed in.

Shadows loomed only a step away. Or a blow…

He sent a silent apology to Mel. To Hell with redemption – he'd rip every demon here into pieces before he'd allow them to hurt her and he'd enjoy it, too. He'd take Hell for eternity if it meant keeping her safe.

He launched his powerful body at the nearest knot of demons. His tail slashed out and sliced through the soft flesh of a throat. Bones crushed beneath the blow from one massive fist as more crunched underfoot. The sibilant rip of parting flesh told him he could drop the arm he'd wrenched off someone's shoulder. No, something's shoulder. Black demon blood sprayed and coated his skin like oil. Luce grinned. The Lord of Hell was born for battle.

Someone was shouting and gesticulating in front of him. He grabbed the noisy head in both hands and wrenched it around until it fell silent. The body fell limp to the carpet.

Something hit his back – a solid blow, but not fast enough. He spun and caught the offending foot, shooting a hand up its owner's shin until he reached the knee. A powerful twist and the lower leg came free. A solid, gory club that he brought down on its former owner's face. It smashed like an egg, leaving no hint in the mess of meat as to who'd been stupid enough to kick the Lord of Hell.

God, it felt good to fight again. For so long, he'd tried to be good for Mel's sake, but he couldn't stand by and let them hurt her. Maybe he was giving his soul to darkness, but it belonged to Mel anyway. Better to lose it in her service than through some stupid mistake of his own.

Two strong arms fastened around his neck from behind, trying to choke him. But the arms were human-sized and couldn't do more than chafe his neck. With the demon still hanging on, he turned, trying to find Mel in the mess of bodies lying at his feet. There. Love flooded through him at the sight of her curled-up body on the coffee table, and he heard the scream of the demon behind him a moment before he smelled burned flesh. His back burned as the demon was blasted away from him, crashing so hard against the wall that it went straight through.

Luce strode through the body parts, not caring how many bones he crushed under his hooves. Melody. Melody. She had to be all right. He'd send the temperature of this room to absolute zero to heal her if he had to. He dropped to his knees beside the coffee table, now the altar that held his beautiful angel's body.

"Won't…let you," a bloodied body panted, digging claws into his side.

Luce flung the dying demon against the wall. It slid down the dalmatian-spotted plaster, leaving a wide streak of equally black blood before it slumped to the floor, no longer moving.

With shaking hands, Luce reached for Mel, not bothering to shift back to his human form. She knew him, no matter what form he took, and he could protect her better like this. "Melody. Please tell me you're all right, Melody. I'll keep you safe." His fingers left a smear of demon blood on her cheek.

She stirred weakly, lifting her eyes to meet his. Hers glistened with tears. "I don't want you to get hurt, my love," she whispered. "Not when pain is what you fear most."

Luce couldn't help it. He grinned. "It was. Now…what's a bit of physical pain compared to the heart-wrenching agony of losing you? I'd fall again – fall a hundred thousand times – if I knew you'd be the one to help me rise in the end."

He slid his arms underneath her and cradled her body carefully to his chest. Now he couldn't help but feel the pain she'd refused to share with him – for every demon she'd burned, she'd felt the same pain that they did, coupled with her despair at harming her colleagues. Only a sweet angel like Melody could feel regret at hurting demons. Her body was worn out with exhaustion and the memory of agony. She was barely holding on to consciousness, her weight sagging against the table beneath her. "I'll protect you from all of them and anyone else," he promised. "Let me take you home."

Mel's eyes closed. Her lips didn't move as her soul said, "Yes, my love. Carry me to Heaven. I can keep you safe there."

No – not Heaven. She couldn't hide in Heaven while she was needed here. They still had to find that crazy little bitch, Persephone.

Speak of the devil. "You really have gone crazy. Good thing we got here when we did – and you still have your pants on."

Stunned, Luce looked down to discover that he'd somehow acquired pants. He didn't own any that fitted his devilish form. Mel – she must have done it. Her faint smile confirmed it.

Persephone continued, "Slaughtering your own minions for fun? What did you do to her?"

Mercifully, the girl was wearing black pants and her cleavage was covered. Luce wished Persephone would wear a burqa around him – there was a first. He shifted so that his body was between her and Mel. He didn't trust her not to hurt Mel in her present fragile state.

"Get away from her!" Persephone shouted, glaring at Luce. Luce glared right back, feeling his fear evaporate in the heat of his fury. How could he have ever feared this skinny girl?

"No," Mel whispered, her fingers tightening

on Luce's arm.

Persephone laid a hand on Mel's shoulder, ripping her fierce gaze from Luce to regard Mel with what Luce thought might be a mix of tenderness and love, edged with panic. "Mel, he's Lucifer, and you're exhausted. We need to get you to Heaven, where you'll be safe and you can recover."

"Make him carry me to Heaven. Face judgement," Mel whispered hoarsely. Her eyelids fluttered.

Luce snorted. Mel must be out of her mind to think he'd go through judgement at Heaven's gates again. If they'd been able to control their own crazies, he and Mel wouldn't be in this mess. They should be thanking him, not judging him, and he'd happily tell them that, too.

Mel's soul-voice didn't sound confused at all. Her tone was calm and strong. "Take me to Heaven, Luce. She doesn't know you can enter with me. I will thank you personally, inside." The fleeting image she sent was enough incentive for him to obey any order she gave. He felt her amusement, though her face betrayed nothing.

"You," Persephone said. "Pick her up. Carefully – I'm already going to cut your willy off for what you've done to her, but you can keep it while you're carrying her, as long as it stays in your pants. You don't want to lose anything else."

Oh Hell. The crazy bitch and the threats he'd forgotten about.

"I won't let her hurt you, Luce," Mel said to his soul.

He'd like to see the nephilim try. He could break her skinny body in two. With exaggerated care, Luce lifted the exhausted angel, wrapping Mel's skirt around her legs so she didn't show her underwear. Mel's eyelids fluttered again and she smiled faintly.

"Take my body to Heaven's gates and keep it alive. Kiss me to wake me when we arrive," Mel's soul said.

Luce grinned. If she wanted a kiss, she'd get one now. Her lips parted beneath his and allowed his tongue entrance. Wait…she wasn't anywhere near as exhausted as she appeared. Mel's soul was as bright as the sun, powerful enough to have taken on the whole roomful of demons without dimming in the slightest. She was up to something, and if he could kiss her for long enough, she'd show him…

"Stop that!" Persephone barked. "You can carry her and that's all. She'll spend a week just brushing her teeth to get the taste of you out of her mouth! I think I'm going to cut your tongue off, too, and give it to Mel to dispose of, so she'll rest assured that you'll never do that again." She pointed at the door. "That way. Get moving." The nephilim continued muttering under her breath, but Luce didn't bother paying attention to her.

He headed out to Reception and came face to face with Hades. "You!"

"You're a crazier bastard than I thought you were," Hades responded, eyeing Mel. "You should have been content with what you had. To think you could touch her without consequences? You'll lose everything and you deserve to. She gave up Hell for you to end the Heavenly War. Gave you your own little domain to bring peace. And this is how you thank her, you arrogant, ungrateful bastard."

Luce's jaw dropped. Mel gave him Hell? Without her, he'd have just been another damned soul in Hell and not its Lord? He reached for her, but couldn't sense her soul near. Somehow, she'd slipped away, leaving her body in his willing arms as he waited for answers. He just needed to get her to Heaven's gates.

"Once the higher angels have reversed whatever you've done to her, she'll be the one you answer to for judgement. But don't expect her to deliver it – she won't soil her hands with you. She'll hand you to the rest of them and they'll want blood for what you've done to her. You won't survive long enough to corrupt another soul and every moment you live will be torment worse than any punishment you've delivered in Hell."

Hades' dark eyes reflected Luce's own. The Lord of Hell and the Lord of the Underworld. Two of the same until Mel changed everything. "That's up to her," Luce grunted, shouldering the other man aside. He had to get Mel to Heaven. Wait, was that…? The touch between them was enough for him to read Hades' soul.

The man thought he'd earn his way into Mel's good graces through this. Maybe she'd even be grateful enough to reward him with wings and a new realm.

"Naming your successor will be up to her, too," Persephone piped up behind him. "When you're gone, Mel will name a new Lord of Hell. Or Lady, if that's her wish." Her giggle set Luce's teeth on edge.

Oh, God, they were both delusional.

"You're after Hell?" Luce snorted. "There's a poisoned chalice. If you're working with Hades, hasn't he told you what it's like to run the Pit of Despair? Dead boring."

Hades' eyes flared with the fires of Tartarus at the insult to the object of his desire.

"Only if you're a demon." She sniffed. "As an angel, the master of Hell wouldn't be confined to the Pit. Heaven, Earth, Hell — all open to them. For you it was a sentence. For anyone else, it's simply an opportunity and a responsibility." She coughed. "At least that's what Mother said, right?"

Mother? Luce whirled around in time to see the silent communication that passed between

Persephone and Hades. "You're talking about that bitch Demeter?"

Hades frowned. "Demeter's one of the gentlest immortals I've ever met, unless you get between her and her children. Then she's a vengeful lioness out for blood." He shuddered as if he had personal experience of this. Luce wondered what the story was. He'd have to ask Mel some time.

"I'll say. She tried to hack my balls off with Michael's sword," Luce said.

"Really?" Persephone giggled.

"Because of your lies," Luce continued. "And Mel sacrificed herself to stop your crazy mother."

"No. NO! I heard you hurt her, not Mother. It was you!" Persephone shouted. "I'll make sure you pay for that, too!"

Luce shrugged. Yes, he regretted hurting Mel, but he'd paid his penance for that, or so Mel had said. He didn't fear her judgement – he was hers to command, and she knew it.

"You'll pay for everything you've done to Mel. And to me!"

"I did nothing to you that you didn't ask

for," Luce replied coolly. "And a lot less than you asked for, as you well know. From what Mel's said, I should have fired you as a PA the same day I hired you. You pestered her constantly with questions while we were away on business. You couldn't even make a dinner reservation without her advice. Do you even remember my favourite entrée? Or after dinner drink? Or where you sent my dry cleaning?"

Persephone pouted. "What do I care? I was just supposed to keep you happy enough to sign your corporation and Hell over to me. If I had to suck your dick a dozen times a day, better me than Mel!" A tear slid down the girl's nose. "Why couldn't you just take what was offered and leave poor Mel alone?"

"I don't expect you to understand," Luce muttered. "And I let you do that once. A single time. And only because you wouldn't leave me alone."

"I told Mel you were gay," Persephone retorted, marching ahead of him.

Gay? He'd slept with men and women, and he'd been both, too. The Lord of Hell seduced anyone and everyone — no matter what it entailed. A labour of lust that he'd even enjoyed at times. But now? There was Mel and only her. As long as Mel took a female form and expressed her preference for his decidedly male body, he could never be gay.

Luce let his laughter ring out across the clouds as they approached Heaven's gates. The nephilim would never understand what Mel meant to him and he'd never let her go.

Forty-three

Unlike the last two times he'd trudged up to these gates, today the benches were empty. The dude in the dress was nowhere to be seen, which Luce figured was a pretty smart move. Someone had warned him that it was a bad day for judging the devil.

The place wasn't entirely deserted, though. Patrick and Koyane stood side by side with three other men, like a row of soldiers at ease on a parade ground. Both Patrick and Koyane acknowledged him with a nod that Luce returned. Neither seemed hostile – more like they were waiting for something.

A figure stepped into view from behind them. Of course. Bloody Michael, with his armour and his sword. Any source of trouble from Heaven and Luce knew Michael had to be involved. If he came anywhere near him or Mel with that flaming sword…

"I've already told him that if he makes any hostile move toward you, you have my permission to shove that sword up his arse," Mel's soul said quietly.

Luce fought to keep his face straight. Mel couldn't be serious.

"I am. But I also advise you not to, as I'll insist that you withdraw the sword and heal him afterwards."

That did take a fair bit of fun out of it.

Persephone cleared her throat. "Right, you. Set her down and back away from her."

Luce waited for Mel's instructions before doing anything with her body.

"On the vacant benches, please, Luce," Mel's soul said. "You'll need your hands free."

Cloud streamed, cool and damp between his

toes as Luce did what she'd asked. He concentrated and caused a cushion to appear beneath Mel's head. The white cotton turned to gold silk before he released his focus.

Luce heard Patrick mutter something, presumably to the man next to him, and they both chuckled quietly.

"I said get away from her!" Persephone insisted, grabbing Luce's hand and yanking on it.

Mel's soul emitted a tiny sigh. "Go with her, Luce. My body is perfectly safe here."

Luce still didn't trust the nephilim. She'd caused too much trouble in the past.

"Read her soul, Luce, like you do mine. Use the hand to hand contact as a conduit. Then you'll know more about her motivations than she does."

Unwillingly, Luce let his fingers close around Persephone's as he poked her soul, just like Mel had told him to. The swirling shadows around the nephilim's soul converged on him, then fled to hide behind the girl's soul instead. That was a first.

"They fear you because you fought them

when they tried to control your soul, my love. You barely had any darkness left to hand to Persi when you signed them over to her." Mel's admiration swelled his heart.

Hesitantly, Luce probed the girl's soul. The contrast to Mel's calm centre was striking. This girl was a whirling storm of contradictions, cycling through frustration, fear, anger and loneliness that Luce recognised. There were frequent flashes of both Demeter and Mel, accompanied by sparks of love that quickly drowned in loneliness and darkness. He didn't understand. He hadn't read enough souls to be able to read any of what the girl's soul told him.

"I'll offer you a deal, demon," Persephone hissed as soon as she'd dragged Luce out of earshot from the others. "If you tell me what you've done to Mel and reverse whatever you've done to my soul, I'll let you keep your…appendages." She eyed his crotch before dragging her gaze up to his face.

Despair tingled across the girl's soul as she thought of herself. She knew she was doomed to never enter Heaven again unless Mel could recover and help her. Even that was only a faint hope.

"Offer her the second but not the first. She'll be in your debt," Mel instructed. Her voice sounded so clear, ringing across the clouds as if she'd spoken aloud. Luce glanced at Mel's body, but it hadn't moved. "I'm beside you, my love, that's why you hear me so clearly."

Luce shrugged. "Mel will tell you herself when she wakes up. I think it's up to her how much she tells you about our delightful time together." He'd picked his seductive tone just right – Persephone blushed redder than Mel ever did. "As for what I've done to you –" he circled her palm with his thumb, just as Mel had done to relax him "– does that mean you're not honouring the deal you made me sign? You don't want everything?"

The girl's soul seemed to collapse under his slight pressure. "I'll give it all back – everything – if you undo what you did to me so that I can enter Heaven again. I'll never be an angel with this darkness haunting me. I'm tainted. Please. Please. I'll do anything." Her pleading voice was so quiet, no one but Luce could hear it. Except Mel.

"Don't agree to accept anything in return. Just take back the dark spirits from her soul," Mel said quietly.

Luce shrank from the very thought of it. Those dark shadows had enslaved his soul for centuries. Kept him out of Heaven and tied him to Hell. Made Mel unreachable. What if they severed the bond between them? He couldn't exist without her now. Someone else had to take them.

Mel continued, "Dark spirits can be vanquished and even destroyed, Luce. You have nothing to fear from them. You've seen me do it and I'm not the only angel who has."

Just because Mel and some other powerful angels could destroy dark, disembodied souls didn't mean he could, Luce fumed. There couldn't be many who knew how – or he'd have seen more angels in Hell.

"Two, Luce," Mel responded, easily reading his thoughts. "Only two angels have done it."

He was willing to bet the other one would require a life of eternal servitude if he asked for a favour of this magnitude. But he'd prefer to put someone else at risk if this went wrong before he'd even think of putting Mel in danger. Maybe his slave master would let him see Mel occasionally…

Mel's laughter hummed so loudly he wondered that Persephone couldn't hear her. "The other angel is you, my love, and the spirits plaguing Persi both witnessed and felt it. Finish the job and you'll be free of them forever. Persi will be eternally in your debt…and you can kiss my body awake so we can end this farce."

The whole exchange took place at the speed of light – too fast for anyone else to have noticed Luce's lapse of concentration. At least, he hoped no one had.

Unfamiliar fear coursed through Luce's body as he looked into Persephone's desperate eyes. For the first time, he pitied her, because he alone knew what she was feeling. And he'd had to wait millennia to meet Mel, the only angel who could save him.

"I'll hold your hand the whole way, my love, and if you falter, I'll burn them into a black hole." Luce felt the warmth of Mel's invisible fingers covering the hand that held Persephone's.

"All right. I'll do it." Persephone sagged in relief, but Luce gritted his teeth as he continued, "You have to block the darkness out of your soul. Curl it up tight and don't let them in, but keep your eyes open." He saw the nephilim's whole body tense up so much she was shaking. Pure panic held her eyes wide.

He had no idea how to entice the souls over to him from Persephone.

"An angel's kiss, my love," Mel informed him.

Luce felt no jealousy or discomfort from her at the thought of him kissing another woman, but he sure felt uncomfortable. He didn't want his lips touching the nephilim. Especially not her mouth. He knew where it'd been.

"It's a soul kiss – the only necessary contact is between your soul and hers. Touching your hand to hers will be more than sufficient." Mel paused as if reading Luce's memory of their own first spectacular kiss on her lounge room floor. When she spoke again, her voice sounded distracted. "Oh. That was…for me. And symbolic, of course, given your motivation for wanting a kiss from me. And…" Her words faded into images and sensations that would make her blush if her soul had been in her body. Mel's carefully hidden desire for him shone through every one.

Luce got the message loud and clear. I love you, too, Mel, he thought as he turned his thoughts to his own soul. Reaching for the girl, then encompassing both her soul and the shadows surrounding it.

Blinding light erupted from him, setting the very air ablaze as the dark souls screeched their torment.

"Burn, baby, burn," he muttered, gritting his teeth as he burned with them. When the pain faded, he knew he'd destroyed them. And it felt damn good.

Mel was one step ahead of him. "Luce, you remember how I asked you to wake me with a kiss…"

He'd give her more than a kiss. The

moment they were alone, he was going to take this incredible buzz and share it with her. All night long and into the next day, at the very least.

Behind him, he heard Persephone fall to her knees. "Thank you," she breathed. "If there's ever any way I can repay you…"

"No worries," Luce replied, waving away her thanks as he strode toward Mel's body. Her soul was already there, waiting for him.

No one stopped him or said a word as he lifted Mel's shoulders and delivered her wake-up kiss. Then another one, just to be sure. And a third seemed to follow almost effortlessly.

"Definitely the sweetest way to wake up. Human fairy tales have that much right. You're an amazing man, Luce, my light of the morning. And a braver one than most. I'll probably be the only one who'll miss…" Mel's soul-voice faded as Luce broke the kiss.

"I'm not leaving you," Luce said, trying to penetrate the thoughts she was slow to hide.

Mel rose. The demon blood on her skin and clothing had vanished, so she glowed in pristine glory. "Lord Lucifer, there is still the matter of your promised judgement," intoned Lady Muriel, her eyes grave as she didn't smile.

Luce glanced at the empty podium in search of the ominous book, but it didn't appear. He folded his arms across his chest and faced her. "I stand by my actions. I'd tear the limbs off every demon in Hell to protect you all over again. A thousand times, if necessary. If that condemns me to Hell, so be it."

"Judgement comes in many forms and this is mine." A murmur rippled through the others but Luce didn't take his eyes off Mel as she wrapped her arms around his neck. "Congratulations, my love," she whispered. A sharp pain told him she'd plucked a feather from his wing before the soft vane brushed against his bare shoulder. Luce glanced down. That couldn't be one of his feathers. It was…

"Whiter than mine, my love," Mel said, fluttering her own beautiful wings into being. The tears in her eyes sparkled as she smiled.

A large hand grasped Luce's forearm in an archaic warrior handshake of sorts. "Brother," a male voice said.

Mel shifted to Luce's side, slipping an arm

across his back as his circled around her waist.

Patrick leaned in and pounded Luce on the back before releasing his arm. "Now we're brothers," he said and Luce nodded, understanding that the white wings had gained him entry into some sort of club.

Koyane bowed, placing his flattened fist over his heart as he repeated, "Brother." Luce returned the gesture.

The three unfamiliar men who'd been standing with them offered similar greetings to Luce, who was dying to ask what club he'd suddenly been accepted into. All five men lined up facing Mel and Luce before offering a deep bow as they chorused, "Lady Muriel."

Ah, that made them Mel's militant fan club, Luce decided. Yeah, he'd be willing to join that, but he needed to set something straight first. He knew what she'd miss and why she hadn't finished her sentence.

Forty-four

"Mel, if you had to choose between the ascent of a soul up the rungs of the angel hierarchy or your own happiness, which would you pick?" Luce asked.

"The soul, of course. I'm happiest when helping another soul achieve its potential," Mel replied.

She couldn't lie, Luce reminded himself. She was telling the truth, because she held her personal happiness less important than another's.

"What choir do these boys belong to?" Luce nodded at the five men who believed they were his brothers.

"Some are Archai, while others are Hashmallim, like me," Mel said slowly. "Why, Luce?"

"I'll never belong to either of those. I'm great at revealing corrupt, useless leaders but hopeless at leading them to choose to do the right thing. If you're hoping I'll be like these guys, you'll be disappointed." He swallowed back his own disappointment, but she needed to know. "The only thing I'm good at is keeping demons in order. Well, as much as anyone can keep demons in order."

Mel smiled up at him as if he was delivering the very best news and not a summary of his own shortcomings.

"The job I do best," he continued, "is the one where I'm the Lord of Hell." He kept his eyes on Mel. "And that job comes with some perks I'm not willing to relinquish." He concentrated hard and was rewarded by Mel's gasp. "The hot body you desire with the dark wings that make me your sexy devil. I wouldn't trade those for anything, because I'll keep those just for you." Luce glanced back to check he'd managed to do it right. Yep, dark feathers on the leading edge, but the trailing edge was cloud-white like a black swan's wings. He kissed the furiously blushing angel whose soul overflowed with gratitude and desire. "I'll trade a perfect soul any day for the imperfect one that you want. All I ever want to be is good enough for you, not someone else's ideal. Yours, forever and always, Melody."

"I love you," was all she managed to say before he kissed her again.

Luce gave her all his attention, so it was some time before he became aware of the voices around them.

"Please, Lord Lucifer, I need to thank you…"

"My daughter, for helping her, I owe you…"

"Must apologise. I didn't realise…"

Luce held tight to Mel as he addressed them all, "I know you all have things you want to say, but it's going to have to wait. Mel's been through a lot tonight and she's overdue some time out in Heaven. So I'll ask you to excuse us…" He lifted Mel into his arms and felt her weight settle comfortably against his chest. Time to make a dramatic re-entry into Heaven. Like he even had to walk through the gates. With Melody in his arms, this devil was already in Heaven.

"You take good care of her, brother."

Luce glanced around and registered that this last came from Patrick, who matched pace with him.

"Mel, you look positively glowing. More radiant than I've ever seen you before. If I didn't know better, I'd think…" Patrick sucked in a breath, his eyes darting from Mel to Luce and back again. He stopped in his tracks. "You're not pregnant, are you?"

Without breaking stride, Luce shot a roguish wink at the saint and grinned.

Forty-five

Hades knew he had to hurry, because that interfering angel Muriel would stop him if she knew what he'd done. He had to get away before she turned her attention to him.

Clouds faded to stone beneath his shoes as he left Heaven's gates behind and reentered the world. She might think she was destroying all the dark souls that had witnessed Lucifer's power, but she'd missed one. One that now coiled almost lovingly around his own corrupt soul – a gift from darling Persephone.

A small shrub had taken root in a crack in the road, a spindly thing that clung precariously to life. It'd be merciful to put an end to its misery, Hades thought, grinning. After all, the human caretakers of this place would poison it soon enough. He reached down and touched it, focussing all his attention in drawing its energy into himself. The plant crumbled into powdery ash at his feet.

Oh, that felt good. Now all he needed was to spread this power to all the dark souls in the Underworld and he'd have an army and power to be reckoned with. Power to take Hell for his own, while that uppity angel Lucifer cavorted in Heaven with Muriel. She wasn't so perfect — she made mistakes just like any human. And it was a grievous error to take Persephone from him. Let's see how powerful she'd be when all Hell broke loose.

His laughter echoed in the darkness and the Underworld trembled.

ABOUT THE AUTHOR

Demelza Carlton has always loved the ocean, but on her first snorkelling trip she found she was afraid of fish.

She has since swum with sea lions, sharks and sea cucumbers and stood on spray drenched cliffs over a seething sea as a seven-metre cyclonic swell surged in, shattering a shipwreck below.

Demelza now lives in Perth, Western Australia, the shark attack capital of the world.

The *Ocean's Gift* series was her first foray into fiction, followed by her suspense thriller *Nightmares* trilogy. She swears the *Mel Goes to Hell* series ambushed her on a crowded train and wouldn't leave her alone.

Want to know more? You can follow Demelza on Facebook, Twitter, YouTube or her website, Demelza Carlton's Place at:

www.demelzacarlton.com

Books by Demelza Carlton

Siren of Secrets series

Ocean's Secret (#1)

Ocean's Gift (#2)

Ocean's Infiltrator (#3)

Siren of War series

Ocean's Justice (#1)

Ocean's Widow (#2)

Ocean's Bride (#3)

Ocean's Rise (#4)

Ocean's War (#5)

How To Catch Crabs

Nightmares Trilogy

Nightmares of Caitlin Lockyer (#1)

Necessary Evil of Nathan Miller (#2)

Afterlife of Alana Miller (#3)

Mel Goes to Hell series

The Devil's Work (#1)

See You in Hell (#2)

Mel Goes to Hell (#3)

To Hell and Back (#4)

The Holiday From Hell (#5)

All Hell Breaks Loose (#6)

The Devil Goes to Heaven (#7)

Romance Island Resort series

Maid for the Rock Star (#1)
The Rock Star's Email Order Bride (#2)
The Rock Star's Virginity (#3)
The Rock Star and the Billionaire (#4)
The Rock Star Wants A Wife (#5)
The Rock Star's Wedding (#6)
Maid for the South Pole (#7)
Jailbird Bride (#8)

Romance a Medieval Fairytale series

Enchant: Beauty and the Beast Retold
Dance: Cinderella Retold
Fly: Goose Girl Retold
Revel: Twelve Dancing Princesses Retold
Silence: Little Mermaid Retold
Awaken: Sleeping Beauty Retold
Embellish: Brave Little Tailor Retold
Appease: Princess and the Pea Retold
Blow: Three Little Pigs Retold
Return: Hansel and Gretel Retold
Wish: Aladdin Retold
Melt: Snow Queen Retold
Spin: Rumpelstiltskin Retold
Kiss: Frog Prince Retold
Reflect: Snow White Retold
Roar: Goldilocks Retold
Cobble: Elves and the Shoemaker Retold